*Johnny Moved Closer
to the Stained-Glass Window . . .*

Before him, lit by the moonlight, was the picture of a gaunt old man in a shimmering blue gown. In one hand the old man held a skull, and in the other a scroll on which the words ZEBULON PATRIARCHA were printed. The old man had wide, hypnotic eyes, and as Johnny stared into them, he heard a faint whispery noise.

Suddenly the old man was standing before him on the dusty floor of the room. Johnny stood paralyzed—he couldn't move a muscle. The old man began to speak, and his words seemed to burst inside Johnny's brain.

I am Zebulon Windrow, said the harsh, grating voice. *You have done great wrong to a member of my family. I seek vengeance, and vengeance I will have. Know that the spirit of Warren Windrow still walks the earth. Be warned, foolish child!*

And with that the old man vanished, and the room was plunged into darkness. . . .

THE REVENGE
OF THE
WIZARD'S GHOST

JOHN BELLAIRS

Frontispiece and map
by Edward Gorey

A BANTAM SKYLARK BOOK®
TORONTO • NEW YORK • LONDON • SYDNEY • AUCKLAND

RL 6, 009–013

*This low-priced Bantam Book
contains the complete text
of the original hard-cover edition.*
NOT ONE WORD HAS BEEN OMITTED.

THE REVENGE OF THE WIZARD'S GHOST
*A Bantam Book / published by arrangement with
Dial Books for Young Readers*

PRINTING HISTORY
Dial edition published November 1985
Bantam Skylark edition / November 1986

*Skylark Books is a registered trademark of Bantam Books, Inc.
Registered in U.S. Patent and Trademark Office and elsewhere.*

Cover art by Edward Gorey, courtesy of Dial Books.

ISBN 0-553-15451-6

Published simultaneously in the United States and Canada

*Bantam Books are published by Bantam Books, Inc. Its trademark, consisting of the
words "Bantam Books" and the portrayal of a rooster, is Registered in U.S. Patent and
Trademark Office and in other countries. Marca Registrada. Bantam Books, Inc., 666
Fifth Avenue, New York, New York 10103.*

PRINTED IN THE UNITED STATES OF AMERICA

CW   0 9 8 7 6 5 4 3 2 1

In memory of my grandfather John Monk

The Revenge of
the Wizard's Ghost

CHAPTER ONE

"No! No! Keep them off me! Keep them off!"

With a sudden jerk Johnny Dixon sat straight up in his bed. He opened his eyes and looked blearily around, and then he wiped his arm across his face, which was wet with tears. Outside, rain was falling steadily, on a September night in the year 1952. Johnny had just awakened from a very unpleasant dream, one that he had had several times before, but each time filled him with sickening fear.

In the dream, Johnny always found himself standing in front of a deserted one-room schoolhouse that stood near a country road, not far from the town of Duston Heights, Massachusetts, where Johnny lived. At first he just stared at the schoolhouse. Then he moved closer, and he noticed a wooden plaque, with Hebrew letters set in a wreath of golden rays, over the door. The door opened, and Johnny went inside. It was cold and dark and musty smelling. At the far end of the room a tall, ornate candlestick stood next to an oblong block that looked like an altar. In the middle of the altar lay a grayish lump, and as Johnny moved closer to see what the thing was, moonlight flooded the room. Glancing quickly to his left, Johnny saw three tall stained-glass windows. The one on the left showed a hooded figure in a long black robe. The face of the figure was completely hidden by the hood, and something that looked like an octopus tentacle dangled from the left sleeve. The window on the right was filled by the menacing shape of an angel dressed like a Roman soldier. He wore a golden breastplate and carried a shield, and in his upraised right hand was a sword of flickering orange flame. The angel's eyes were wide and unearthly, and they were staring relentlessly at Johnny. They seemed to be burning holes in his brain. With a violent effort, Johnny tore his eyes away from the angel's gaze and looked at the middle window. Before him, lit by the moonlight, was the picture of a gaunt old man in a shimmering blue gown. In one hand the old man held a skull, and in the other a scroll on which the words ZEBULON PATRIARCHA were printed. Like the angel, the old man had wide, hypnotic eyes, and as Johnny stared into them, he heard a faint whispery noise. Suddenly the old man was standing before him on the dusty floor of the room.

Johnny stood paralyzed—he couldn't move a muscle. The old man began to speak, and his words seemed to burst inside Johnny's brain.

I am Zebulon Windrow, said the harsh, grating voice. *You have done great wrong to a member of my family. I seek vengeance, and vengeance I will have. Know that the spirit of Warren Windrow still walks the earth. Be warned, foolish child!*

And with that the old man vanished, and the room was plunged into darkness. Instantly Johnny heard a horrible rustling sound, like the fluttering of a million insect wings, echoing all around him. Feelers brushed across his body and his face, and he began frantically waving his arms and yelling. The angry buzzing got louder and louder. Johnny woke up.

The September rain kept falling. Johnny closed his eyes and swallowed hard. He shuddered and opened his eyes, groping for his glasses, which lay neatly folded on the bedside table. Finally he found them and put them on.

Johnny was thirteen years old. He was short, blond-haired, and pale, and a bit on the timid side. Johnny's mother was dead and his father was an officer in the Air Force, so for almost two years Johnny had been living with his grandparents. This was an unusual arrangement, but Johnny was an unusual kid. The only boy his own age he really got along with was Byron Ferguson, or Fergie, as he was usually called. Johnny's best friend in all the world was an elderly man who lived across the street, a history professor named Roderick Childermass. The two of them were very close, and they had shared some strange adventures since Johnny had first come to Duston Heights. One of these incidents occurred last February, when Johnny and the professor were staying at a country inn in New Hampshire. Accidentally, the professor had touched a tiny skull that was inside a dollhouse room, and this had awakened an ancient curse that had been dormant many years. It was a spell laid on the Childermass family by a man named Warren Windrow, who was hanged in the 1850s because he had tried to murder the professor's granduncle, Lucius Childermass. With Johnny's help, the professor had been saved from destruction and, supposedly, the curse was broken. But was it? Johnny wanted to believe that everything was all right. But why was he having this horrible dream, over and over?

As he walked the streets of Duston Heights that September, Johnny thought a lot about the dream. He thought of telling the professor about it, but the professor would probably say that Johnny was merely suffering from some bad feelings caused by the awful experience that he had had. Johnny knew that this was probably a reasonable thing to say. After all, he had read about people who had nightmares because of things that happened to them, like bad car accidents. Johnny also thought about what Fergie would say if he told him about the dreams. Fergie was a smart-alecky type. He would just tell Johnny not to eat so many salami-and-pickle sandwiches. So after he had chewed the matter over in his mind for a while, Johnny told himself that he wouldn't talk about the dreams to anybody. He didn't want his friends to laugh at him, and anyway, the dreams would go away eventually.

At the end of September it got warm and hazy. One evening Johnny and the professor were sitting out on the professor's front porch. They had played several games of chess and eaten about half of a chocolate layer cake with banana-fudge frosting, and now they were just relaxing and listening to the feeble chirping of the last few crickets. The professor was sitting in an old saggy wicker chair. His feet were up on the porch rail and he was puffing at one of his smelly Balkan Sobranie cigarettes. Professor Childermass was a short man with a wild mess of white hair on his head and a nose that looked like an overripe strawberry. His normal expression was crabby, and he did indeed have a rotten temper, but he was also very kindhearted and a good friend to those who got to know him well. He took the cigarette out of his mouth and turned to Johnny, who was rocking lazily back and forth on the porch swing.

"The last gasp of summer, eh, John Michael?" said the professor. "Pretty soon we'll be raking leaves till our arms get tired, and then we'll be shoveling snow and cursing the foul weather. At least *I'll* be cursing—I usually find something to gripe about in any kind of weather, being the foul-tempered old coot that I am."

A pause. No response. The swing creaked gently as Johnny swayed back and forth in it.

The professor frowned. He was beginning to get concerned. He knew that Johnny got moody sometimes, but usually he could see the boy's foul moods coming a mile off. And this evening Johnny had been very cheerful and talkative—until now, anyway.

The professor coughed. "Well, John!" he said loudly. "Another baseball season has gone by, and once again the Red Sox have been left in the lurch. But that's life, isn't it? By the way, what's on your mind besides hair? Hmm? You haven't said a blessed word for the last ten minutes. Did my cake clog up your windpipe? Are you choking to death quietly and with great dignity? Eh?"

"I'm okay, professor," said Johnny at last. His voice sounded strained, as if he had to make an effort to speak.

"You don't *sound* okay," muttered the professor, giving Johnny a quick sidelong glance. "Remember, John, if there's something eating you, it's better to talk about it. I'm no psychiatrist, but I am your friend, and we've always trusted each other before—that's what friendship is all about, isn't it? Please don't sit there with something unpleasant bottled up inside you. Bring it out into the open! You'll feel better, I promise!"

Johnny shifted uncomfortably in his seat, and it seemed as if he were about to say something. But then, through the open window behind them, came the sound of the mantel clock striking. It binged ten times.

"My gosh, it's ten o'clock!" exclaimed Johnny as he slid quickly off his seat. "I have to get up early tomorrow for school. Thanks for the cake and . . . and everything." As the professor stared, Johnny dashed across the porch, down the steps, and halfway down the walk. But then, suddenly, he turned.

"Do you believe in dreams, professor?" he yelled, cupping his hands to his mouth.

The professor was astonished. "Do I . . ." he began in a wondering voice. Then he jumped to his feet, but Johnny did not wait for an answer. He raced across the street into the darkness, and the professor heard the screen door of the Dixon house slam.

"*Blast!*" exclaimed the professor as he flung down his cigarette and ground it under the sole of his shoe. "If that doesn't just beat everything!"

By midnight everyone on Fillmore Street was asleep. The temperature had dropped sharply, and fog began to drift into the town. It slithered past the Dixon house in ghostly curls and eddies, and one long gray finger of mist rose up to touch the half-open window of the room where Johnny lay asleep. Suddenly Johnny sat up. With wide-open, unseeing eyes he turned his head, peeled back the sheet, and slid out of bed. Moving stiffly, he walked out of the room, down the front stairs, and out onto the sidewalk. It was a chilly night, and he was wearing only thin cotton pajamas—nevertheless, he did not seem to feel the cold. Down the foggy street he went, walking for blocks and blocks, till he came to the edge of town. He crunched over the gravel that bordered a narrow blacktop road, but if the gravel hurt his bare feet, he didn't notice. Suddenly he stopped. Off to the right, in a weedy yard, was an old white schoolhouse with boarded windows. Stumping along woodenly, like a robot, Johnny made his way through the woods to the front steps of the school, and then—noiselessly—the old weathered door opened. Johnny disappeared inside for a fairly long time. When he came out again, his face still looked blank and his eyes were glazed. But his mouth was twisted into a harsh, brutal, sneering smile. The smile distorted Johnny's face, and almost made him look like a different person.

When Johnny woke up the next morning, he made a shocking discovery. His pajama bottoms were damp from the knees down and his feet were dirty. There was gravel on his sheets, and there were gravelly footprints on the floor of his bedroom. What on earth had happened? Had he been walking in his sleep? It certainly looked like it, but where had he been to? Johnny felt panicky at first, and then, when he had calmed down a bit, he wondered what his grandmother would say about the dirty sheets and the footprints on the floor. As he sat thinking about this, someone knocked on the door. With a sinking heart Johnny got up to answer it. There Gramma stood, with a broom in one hand and a dustpan in the other. She did not seem to be in a very good mood.

"John Dixon," she said in an accusing tone, "can you tell me anything about these footprints an' this dirt I been sweepin' up on the front stairs? Hmm?"

Johnny swallowed hard. "I guess I must've been walkin' in my sleep, Gramma," he said weakly.

Gramma looked startled, and then her frown turned to a kindly smile. "I shoulda guessed," she said, shaking her head. "My uncle Martin used ta walk in his sleep, an' it nearly drove his wife crazy. Well, look. You hafta get ready fer school, so get on down t' the bathroom an' wash up. Only tonight remember t'lock your bedroom door before you turn in. That'll keep you in—leastways that's what people claim. Now go on, get a move on!"

Johnny ran quickly down the hall to the bathroom and heaved a deep sigh of relief. But as he brushed his teeth, the nagging questions came back. *Why had he been walking in his sleep? And where had he gone?*

As the days of October passed, Johnny began to behave strangely. He took long walks by himself, and he found that he was thinking about some very peculiar things. He thought about bags of gold dust, and men panning for gold in mountain streams. He kept playing poker games in his mind, and he would mutter things like *Four of a kind beats a full house. . . . See you, and raise you twenty dollars. . . . Pair of jacks bets.* He thought of gold coins and silver dollars clattering on tables in smoky, dimly lit saloons. He thought about grizzled, sunburned men who carried long-barreled six-shooters in leather holsters, and he thought about knife fights too. Sometimes, on these long lonely walks, Johnny would feel himself getting very angry. He was angry at a smug, superior-acting young bearded man who always won at cards and threw money around as if it meant nothing to him. But who was this man? Johnny hadn't the slightest idea.

At night Johnny began to have dreams that were even more frightening than the ones he had been having before. In these dreams he was led out onto a rough wooden stage with a trapdoor out in the middle. Down below the edge of the stage, Johnny saw a sea of upturned faces, men and women who sneered and mocked and laughed at him. His arms were tied behind him and someone was shoving him out onto the middle of the platform. He tried to struggle, but it was no use. He was standing on the trapdoor, and someone was lashing his feet together with a leather strap. The noose dangled overhead, and he saw it drop lower and felt the rough, hairy rope around his neck. The noose tightened, and a black sack was dropped over his head. Johnny began to scream, and then he was falling, falling. . . .

Johnny would wake up in a state of panic, with a feeling of tightness around his throat. Whenever Johnny had this dream, he found that it was impossible to go to sleep again that night.

People began to notice that there was something the matter with Johnny. He would show up at the breakfast table with a wild, haunted look on his face, and his grandmother and grandfather would glance at each other in a frightened way, and they would ask if he felt all right. Johnny would snap at them and say that of course he felt all right, and that would end the conversation. In school Johnny was doing badly. Usually he did very well in subjects like Latin, history, English, and science—Johnny was a real brain. But now his mind went blank when he tried to read or answer test questions. And when he attempted to concentrate on homework, a voice would whisper in his ear and tell him to forget about his work, it wasn't really important. This whispering, insistent voice was with Johnny much of the day now. When he was with his friend Fergie, it would ask him why he spent so much time with this ugly, gawky oaf. When he was with the professor, it would tell him that an old man was a rather strange companion for a young, handsome lad like himself. Johnny didn't always listen to the voice, or obey it—in fact, he tried hard to fight the whisperer and make him go away. But as time went by, he began to get the horrible feeling that there was somebody else inside him, someone who was trying to take over.

One windy evening in the middle of October, Johnny and his friend Fergie were over at the professor's house for a card party. Fergie was a gangly kid with a droopy face and a long, blunt-ended nose. He had big ears and big feet, and he was always making jokes. Johnny had met Fergie a year ago at Boy Scout camp, and they had become friends quickly. Fergie had gotten to know the professor through Johnny, and now the three of them often did things together. The card party turned out to be a lot of fun for the two boys and the old man. They drank lots of hot spiced cider and gorged on Rigo Jancsi, which is a kind of super chocolate torte with two kinds of flavored whipped cream and fondant frosting on top. They did all their gobbling in the kitchen, and then they took their cider mugs out to the dining room and sat down to play hearts. As they played, the professor was watching Johnny closely. He knew that there was something wrong with Johnny and he was trying to figure out what it was. Oddly enough, Johnny wanted to tell the professor about his problems—but he was scared to. The voice inside him told Johnny that awful things would happen to him if he tried to talk to the old man, so he just clammed up.

In the middle of the game a peculiar thing happened. The professor led with the king of clubs, Johnny threw on a jack, and Fergie laid down the four.

Johnny's eyes grew wide. "The four of clubs!" he exclaimed. "That's the devil's bedposts! It's bad luck!"

The professor's mouth dropped open. "The devil's *bedposts*? Where in the name of Ned did you dig up *that* expression?"

Johnny shrugged. "Where I come from, they say it all the time," he muttered.

Fergie opened his mouth to say something, but he saw the fierce glare on Johnny's face, so he said nothing. The game went on in silence for some time, but finally the professor decided that he had had enough. He was angry and puzzled, and he also felt hurt.

"John," he said, throwing his cards down suddenly on the table, "I have really had about all that I can take from you! You seemed to be having a good time earlier this evening, and then you turned into a Gloomy Gus. I just don't get it!" Tears came to the professor's eyes. He was really very upset. "John," he said in a trembling voice, "I *thought* that I was your friend. You always used to tell me your troubles. Why won't you tell me now?"

Johnny laid his cards down on the table in front of him. He stared at the professor, and a change came over his face. His eyes grew hard and his lips curled into a sneer. "Because you're a *Childermass!*" he said hatefully. "And they are the *enemy!*"

As the professor and Fergie watched in utter astonishment, Johnny reached out and, with a swipe of his hand, knocked his mug of cider over. Then he shoved his chair back, jumped up, and ran out of the house, slamming the front door behind him.

CHAPTER TWO

The sound of the slammed door seemed to hang in the still air of the dining room. Fergie and the professor stared at each other and then at the brownish pool of cider that lay in the middle of the table.

"Good God!" exclaimed the professor at last. "I would never have *believed* that he could behave that way! If you had told me about it, I would have figured that you were lying! What on earth do you think is happening to him?"

Fergie shook his head glumly. "You got me, professor! The other day when we were eatin' ice cream down at Peter's Sweet Shop, he just started gettin' red in the face for no reason at all. I asked him what was wrong, an' he told me to shut up. An' then on the way out, he saw a box of matches on the counter an' he called them *loco focos*. 'What?' I said. 'They're *loco focos*,' he said. 'That's what they're called.' Whaddaya make of it, prof? Is he goin' outa his jug?"

The professor heaved a deep sigh. "I don't know, Byron. For the life of me, I don't. But look, let's get some wet rags and clean up this glop. We can discuss this matter later."

As Fergie and the professor were wiping the table, the doorbell rang. The professor's heart leaped. Maybe it was Johnny. Maybe he had come back to apologize and explain that his behavior was all part of some insane practical joke. But when he went to open the door, the professor found Grampa Dixon standing there. He was a tall, gangly man in a gray work shirt, gray wash pants, and an unbuttoned tweed overcoat. A flat, paper-wrapped package was sticking out of one of the overcoat's pockets. A few wisps of white hair still clung to the old man's freckled head, and he wore gold-rimmed glasses. The flesh of his face was loose and wrinkly, but his eyes were bright and alert. At the present moment he looked very, very unhappy.

"Hi, Rod," he said, smiling faintly. "Can . . . can I talk to you for a minute?"

The professor gave Grampa a hard look. "Is it about Johnny?" he asked.

Grampa was startled. "Yeah . . . how'd you guess?"

The professor smiled sourly. "I have a crystal ball," he said sarcastically. "Sure, come on in. Byron and I are just cleaning up a . . . uh, an accident. It won't take us long to finish here. Why don't I pour a glass of port for you and me and some more hot cider for Byron? I suspect that we have a good deal to talk about."

A few minutes later the three of them were in the professor's living room. Fergie was sitting in an armchair, and Grampa was on the sofa. The professor was standing in front of the fireplace with his arms folded, and he looked the way he did when he was conducting one of his classes at the local college. He had just finished telling Grampa about the strange way that Johnny had behaved this evening.

". . . and so," the professor went on, glancing nervously around the room, "I think we will all agree that there is something wrong with Johnny. But what is it? What strange disease could he possibly be suffering from?"

"I dunno," said Grampa wearily, "but I found somethin' in his room that really might help us figure the whole thing out. It's over there in my overcoat."

Grampa's coat was draped across one of the living-room chairs. The professor walked over and slid the flat, brown-paper parcel from one of the frayed pockets. Moving to the coffee table, he knelt down and began to unwrap the package while the other two watched. Inside were a cracked glass photographic plate and a gold coin. The photograph showed an unpleasant young man with long, stringy blond hair. There were creases and lines on the man's face, and his mouth was drawn down into a sullen scowl. His eyes were hard and cold, and an ugly scar ran across the bridge of his nose and partway down one cheek. The man was wearing an old-fashioned high white collar with a wide black silk tie that was done up in a bow. As for the coin, it was rather plain and homely. On one side the initials JSO were stamped, and the words UNITED STATES OF AMERICA ran around the rim. On the other side was the phrase 5 DOLLS inside a border of little stars.

The professor glanced up at Grampa. "Henry, where on earth did you get these things?"

The old man looked sheepish. "I found 'em in the top drawer o' Johnny's dresser. I know I shouldn't've been pokin' around in there, but I was lookin' for my jack-knife an' I wondered if he had borrowed it. Where the heck d'ye think he got this stuff?"

The professor frowned. "Where indeed? As for the picture, I would say that it was taken around the time of the Civil War, or maybe a little bit earlier. And the coin . . . well, Byron, you collect coins. Did you ever see one like this?"

Fergie picked up the coin and turned it over. He held it up to the light and squinted at it. "Gee . . . I dunno, professor," he said at last. "I'm not rich enough to have any gold coins in my collection, but maybe . . . Heck, this looks like it might be one o' those gold coins that they minted out in California durin' the Gold Rush. A lota businessmen had their own coin-makin' machines, an'—"

"Oh, my good Lord!" exclaimed the professor, cutting him off. A look of amazement and horror spread across his face. "You don't suppose—"

The phone rang.

In panicky haste the professor scrambled to his feet, tripped over a stool, and stumbled over to the phone table in the corner. He picked up the receiver and found that he was listening to Gramma Dixon. She was talking a mile a minute and it was obvious that she was scared half out of her mind.

"Madam, madam, please try to calm down!" said the professor irritably. "I can hardly make out a word that you're saying!"

"Calm *down!*" exclaimed Gramma indignantly. "You come over here an' see what's happened to Johnny an' then see if *you* can calm down! Just you see if you can!" She began to cry.

The professor's face turned pale. "We'll be over right away," he said in a low voice. He hung up and turned to face the other two, who were sitting with their mouths open, staring at him.

A short while later, the professor, Gramma, Grampa, and Fergie were all up in Johnny's bedroom. The reading lamp on the bureau was on and it cast a pale glow over Johnny, who lay still on the bed. He was wearing all his clothes, even his shoes; his eyes were shut and he was breathing heavily. His face had turned a coppery yellow, and around his neck was an angry red welt, like the mark of a rope. His mouth was curled down into an ugly sneer, and across the bridge of his nose ran a scar mark that had never been there before. Johnny's whole face was strangely distorted, and if he had not been wearing his glasses and his usual clothes, the four people in the room might not have known who he was.

For a long time nobody spoke. Gramma held her apron to her face and sobbed softly, but that was the only sound in the room. Finally the professor spoke.

"How . . . how long has he been like this?" he asked in a tight, strained voice.

Gramma lowered the apron, showing her red eyes and tear-stained face. "I . . . I heard him come in a while ago," she said, sniffing, "an' he went straight up to his room an' slammed the door. I come upstairs a little bit after that, an' I was gonna knock on his door t'see if he was okay, only all of a sudden I heard this voice inside his room. 'Twasn't his voice, it was somebody else's. So I got scared becuz I figgered a robber had got in, an' I was gonna go call the police, but then I said to myself, 'Heck, it's jist the radio,' so I went back an' knocked, an' Johnny didn't answer, so I opened the door, an' . . ." Gramma broke down and started crying again. She just couldn't go on.

"Oh, my gosh," wailed Grampa as he shook his head slowly. "What're we gonna do? What in the name of God can we do? Can you think of anyone who can help us? Should I call the doctor?"

The professor laid his hand on Grampa's arm. "No. Don't call the doctor . . . not just yet, anyway. There's somebody we ought to contact first: my old friend Father Higgins."

Grampa closed his eyes and put his hands to his face. To him, calling a priest meant only one thing: the Last Rites, the special ceremony that a Catholic priest performs for people who are dying. "Is . . . is it as bad as all that?" he said through his fingers.

"No, no, no!" snapped the professor. "I didn't mean what you think I meant. No—there's another reason why I need to speak to Father Higgins."

Grampa looked puzzled. Then he said, "Is there anything we can do? Right now, I mean, for Johnny?"

The professor bit his lip. "Yes. Yes, there is: Go find a crucifix. You are devout Catholics—you must have one in the house. Find one and put it in Johnny's room." He turned to Fergie. "And as for you, Byron," he went on, "I think you had better head for home. There's nothing more you can do here, for the time being, and your mom will have a fit if you're out too late. If your folks ask about Johnny, tell them he's sick."

Fergie turned to the professor and glared at him. "Look, prof," he said bitterly, "I'm Johnny's best friend, so if you don't mind, would you please tell me what the heck is wrong with him?"

The professor's eyes met Fergie's. "Have you ever heard of *possession* by the devil, Byron?" he asked grimly. "And do you remember the ghost of Warren Windrow? You're a bright boy; you can put two and two together. Now please go home, go home and pray. I'll call you later."

Fergie went home, and the professor went downstairs to call Father Higgins. They talked for a long time, and the priest said that he'd be over as soon as he could possibly get there. When the professor stepped into the hall, he found Grampa waiting for him.

"What did he say?" he asked breathlessly. "Is he gonna help us?"

The professor sighed. "He says he's going to try. Henry, you heard the hints that I dropped to Fergie, so you may as well know what I think, if you haven't guessed already. The evil spirit of Warren Windrow has come back, and it has taken possession of Johnny's body. That photograph is almost certainly a photograph of him—I read in my granduncle Lucius's diary that Warren Windrow had a scar on his nose and a sneering mouth. And that coin from the Gold Rush days in California a hundred years ago—don't you see, it all fits! I know it sounds bizarre and unlikely, but it's the best explanation for what has been happening. So I've called in Father Higgins, and he is going to try to cast the evil spirit out. He says he's never done anything like this before, but he told me he'd try, and that is all that I can ask." The professor's eyes filled with tears, and his voice began to crack. "I hope it works," he added, shaking his head. "God, how I hope it works!"

CHAPTER THREE

Later that same night a small group of worried, frightened people gathered in Johnny's bedroom. Near the head of the bed stood Gramma, Grampa, and the professor. At the foot of the bed was Father Higgins. He was a tall man in a black suit with a stiff white clerical collar; around his shoulders was draped a narrow band of purple silk with black crosses stitched on it. In his hands the priest held a small black book, and as he made the Sign of the Cross in the air above the bed, he said; "*Adjutorium nostrum in nomine Domini.*" The Latin words meant, *Our help is in the name of the Lord.* The professor gave the correct reply: "*Qui fecit coelum et terram*"—*Who made the heaven and the earth.*

On and on ran the Latin phrases. Sometimes the priest

would stop and pick up a silver holy-water container that lay on a table nearby, and he would sprinkle the bed and then go on reading. Johnny lay perfectly still. He was now wearing his best pair of flannel pajamas, and he was tucked in between the clean sheets, his hands folded on the blanket. His face still had that ugly distorted look, and the livid red lines on his neck and nose had not gone away. Father Higgins continued to read. Finally the priest closed the book and laid it down. He reached into his jacket pocket and took out a small silver cross that hung from a chain of tiny silver links. At the place where the arms of the cross met was a tiny crystal bubble, and under it were two splinters from the True Cross, the cross Jesus died on. Father Higgins stepped around the end of the bed and moved toward Johnny, holding the cross and chain in both hands. But just as he bent to put the chain around Johnny's neck, something happened.

Johnny's eyes flew open. They bulged from his head and his face turned red. He made choking noises in his throat and the red line around his neck turned to a ghastly purple. Suddenly a harsh, grating voice was heard—it seemed to come out of the air over Johnny's bed, and it said, *"Move back. I will choke the life out of him if you bring that thing near. In the name of Azoth, aroint ye! Begone!"*

Horrified, the priest stepped back. Hastily he stuffed the cross and chain into his pocket, and he crossed himself rapidly while muttering a prayer.

"I'm sorry, my friends," he said with a helpless shrug. "There's nothing more I can do. There are forces here that are just too strong for me."

Gramma and Grampa hung their heads. The professor swore helplessly and clenched and unclenched his fists. The red faded from Johnny's cheeks, and his eyes closed, and the choking noises stopped. He looked just the way he had looked before the exorcism began.

Gramma spoke in a husky, choked-up voice. "Do . . . do you think he'll . . . die, father?"

The priest shook his head. "I don't know, Kate. I just don't know. I think that—for the time being—we better get him down to the hospital. They'll put a tube in his arm and feed him intravenously, and that'll keep him alive—unless the evil spirit has other ideas."

A low chuckle was heard in the room, and everyone shivered.

An ambulance took Johnny to Hannah Duston Hospital, and a feeding tube was put in his arm. He was examined by doctors and nurses, who drew blood and took his temperature and listened to his heart. Everyone was shocked by his appearance, but no one could come up with any good reason why he looked that way. Nobody tried to tell the people at the hospital that Johnny was possessed by an evil spirit—the doctors would have laughed at an explanation like that. At last they decided that he was suffering from "an unknown illness of the brain," which meant that they really didn't know what was wrong with him. Days passed, and Johnny's condition stayed the same. The professor came to the hospital to visit, and so did Gramma and Grampa and Fergie and Father Higgins. Much of the time the professor felt helpless, and he hated to feel that way, so he took several trips up to Durham, New Hampshire, to visit Professor Charles Coote, an old friend of his. Professor Coote was an expert on magic, and he had read many books on demons and ghosts. Professor Childermass hoped that he would get some sort of help from his old friend—at least he would feel as if he were trying.

One night, about a week after Johnny had been taken to the hospital, Professor Childermass was driving back from Durham. He had had another long conversation with his old pal, and they had come up with some ideas that Professor Coote thought might be helpful in their battle against the evil spirit that had taken possession of Johnny's body. Professor Childermass had his doubts. He was becoming very depressed about the whole business, and as he sped along Route 125, his mind was full of gloomy and hate-filled thoughts. By the time he reached Duston Heights, he was feeling extremely cranky, and he knew that if he went straight home he would end up throwing dishes around and cursing at the top of his voice. So he decided to see how Johnny was getting along. Visiting hours at the hospital were over, but he could at least ask how the poor kid was doing.

When Professor Childermass walked into the front lobby of the hospital, he knew immediately that something strange was going on. Nurses and interns were standing around in little groups, talking excitedly. A doctor was standing near the reception desk, and he was trying to answer some questions that a short man in a trench coat was firing at him. The professor recognized the short man—it was Eddie Gumpert from the local newspaper. Puzzled, the professor walked to the reception desk, where a frightened-looking young nurse was sitting.

"Excuse me, ma'am," said the professor crisply, "but I wonder if you could tell me anything about the condition of Johnny Dixon. He's in room—"

The nurse's eyes grew wide. "Johnny *Dixon?*" she said in a voice that was almost a shriek. "Oh. Oh, my. Well, it's odd that you should mention him, because . . . well, you see these people, well, they're all talking about Johnny, because . . . because . . ."

At this point the professor felt a heavy hand on his shoulder, and a rumbly voice said, "Hi, prof! How's it goin'?" It was Doc Schermerhorn, the Dixons' family physician. He was a fat, shambly man who used bad grammar and told lousy jokes. The professor did not like Doc Schermerhorn—in fact, he could hardly stand to be in the same room with him. But now, as he turned toward the man, the professor tried hard to act polite. Doc Schermerhorn had been taking care of Johnny and he might possibly have some information.

"Hello, Carl," said the professor with a forced smile. "Nice to see you. Look, can you tell me anything about

Johnny? This place seems to be in a state of total chaos!"

Doc Schermerhorn grinned and winked knowingly. "Heck, prof," he said cheerily, "you come along at just the right time. Johnny's all right!"

The professor's jaw dropped. "He's . . . all *right*? You mean . . ."

Doc Schermerhorn nodded. "He's fit as a fiddle! It happened all of a sudden, coupla hours ago. Nobody knows why he got better, but then nobody knows why he got sick, either. It's weird."

The professor was still stunned. A hundred ideas came whirling into his head, but none of them made any sense. "Well, then, can I . . . can I go up and see him?" he asked.

Doc Schermerhorn shrugged. "Don't see why not. C'mon, I'll take you up t'see him. An' I wantcha to see somethin' else too. Y'see, Johnny . . . well, he kinda wrecked his room when he got better. They got him in another room now, but I wantcha to see the room he was in. There's somethin' on the wall—darnedest thing. He must've done it, only they can't figger out how. Can't even find the crayon he did it with. I'll show ya— see what *you* make of it."

Doc Schermerhorn led the professor to an elevator. They went up to the second floor and walked down a whitewashed corridor. Outside one door they halted, and Doc Schermerhorn knocked. No one answered, so the doctor pushed the door open and let the professor go in first. The room was certainly a mess: The bedside table had been tipped over, and a heap of broken glass lay on the floor. The curtains were pulled down, and there were long rips in a white cloth screen that stood near the bed. The pictures on the walls had been knocked crooked, and big holes had been punched in them. But one thing in the room drew the professor's attention immediately. On the white wall near the bed that Johnny had been in, huge words had been scrawled. The writing covered the whole wall, and ended with a flourish that ran halfway across the ceiling. At first the professor could not figure out what the enormous, scraggly words said, but after a little staring, he understood: They said, *I GIVE HIM BACK TO YOU.*

CHAPTER FOUR

Johnny had been saved. He had to stay in the hospital a few days longer while the doctors checked him over, but after that he went home. He seemed to be in great shape. His eyes were clear, and the awful red marks were gone from his neck and nose. His heart was beating at the proper speed, and his temperature was normal. There was great rejoicing on Fillmore Street when Johnny arrived. The Dixons' parlor was full of bouquets of flowers that had been sent by his high school teachers, and there were get well cards from everybody who knew him. Father Higgins stopped by to see how he was, and so did Professor Coote, who had driven all the way from New Hampshire to see his favorite bookworm.

And the professor threw a big welcome-home party for Johnny, with punch and Halloween candies and a big cake with orange-and-black icing. For the moment everything seemed fine, and Johnny's only problem was people who kept asking him questions like "Are you *sure* you really feel all right?"

After a couple of days at home Johnny went back to school, and the uproar over his recovery began to die down. Everything seemed to be returning to normal, everything seemed fine—or did it? One person was not at all satisfied, and that was Professor Childermass. He just could not believe that the ghost of Warren Windrow had left Johnny's body for good. Why had the ghost left? It didn't make any sense. Exorcism hadn't worked; they hadn't even been able to get near Johnny with the silver crucifix. The ghost had been cold, merciless, and cruel—not the sort of creature from whom you would expect compassion. So the professor was still nervous and watchful. He started reading books about ghosts. The more he read, the more he thought, and one night he called up Professor Coote to ask him to research everything he could find out about the Windrow family.

"After all," he said, "they were a family of wizards and witches. And maybe one of them left behind some talisman or amulet that could help us if that evil creature decides to return."

"Well, Roderick," said Professor Coote wearily, "I'll poke about in libraries and graveyards and family records and see what I can discover. But do you really think that all this worrying is necessary? What makes you think the ghost is planning another attack?"

The professor was silent a moment. "I really don't know why I'm so worried, Charley," he said at last. "It's just instinct, I guess. Have you ever seen a cat playing with a mouse before he kills it? He lets it think it might escape, and then, just as the poor thing imagines that it's in the clear, whammo! The cat pounces and tears the mouse to bits. And *that*, my dear friend, is the sort of thing I'm worried about. The ghost might think it was great sport to let Johnny go—for a while."

"Heaven help us!" said Professor Coote in a worried voice. "I hope you're wrong!"

"So do I," said his friend. "So do I!"

November was a rainy, windy month. Johnny was back in his usual everyday routine, and nothing bad seemed to be happening to him. But he felt strange, because he could not figure out why he had landed in the hospital. No one would tell him anything. The professor would only say that he had "been through a bad time," and Gramma and Grampa were strangely silent too. Johnny could remember some of the frightening dreams that he had, but there were big gaps in his memory: For instance, he could not remember anything that had happened to him on the night he went to the card party at the professor's house. And there was another odd thing: The day after he got home from the hospital, Father Higgins showed up at his house and gave him the silver cross to wear. He told Johnny to put the chain around his neck and wear it all the time, even in bed at night and in the bathtub. When Johnny asked why, Father Higgins clammed up. So Johnny wore the cross, but one day he found that the clasp on the chain was irritating his neck. He tried to take the chain off, and the clasp broke. Johnny stuffed the cross and chain into a vase on his bureau and he promised himself that he would get the clasp fixed right away. In the meantime he'd just have to take his chances with whatever bad luck happened to come his way.

One gusty cold night Johnny was walking home from Fergie's house. At the start of the walk he was in a pretty good mood, because he had beaten Fergie in three straight games of chess. But as he walked on, he found that he was getting jittery. It was so windy that a few dead branches came clattering down near Johnny, and sometimes a very strong gust would knock over a garbage can in an alley. The endless moaning in the trees was not very pleasant either. By the time he got to the end of Fillmore Street, Johnny was jumping at every sound that he heard. He glanced ahead and saw the windows glowing in his grandparents' house, and—as always—this sight made him feel good. He started walking faster, but he came to a sudden halt when he heard a scraping noise off to his right.

Something was moving toward him. Johnny jumped, and then he looked and heaved a sigh of relief. It was just a paper plate, sliding across the street. Or was it? As Johnny stood watching, the plate scuttled closer, and he saw that it was not a plate at all. It was a mask. Was it a Halloween mask that some kid had thrown away? No, it did not seem to be that kind of mask: It was completely white, and there were no eyeholes or mouth hole. The mask looked like a plaster cast that had been made of somebody's face—somebody's dead face. It was the face of a young man with a scar across his nose and a sneering, brutal mouth. A cold breath blew over Johnny's body. Where had he seen the face before? Dim memories of an old photograph flashed through his mind, and horror began to creep over him. He edged away from the ghastly thing and started to run, and he didn't stop till he was in his front hall with the door closed behind him.

The next day, on his way to school, Johnny searched in the gutter and in the front yards near his house. But he did not find the mask. *Forget about it!* he said to himself as he marched off to school—but that was easier said than done. It was a long time before he could get the ugly, pale mask out of his mind.

Months passed and Johnny went on feeling fine. He passed his first-semester exams easily, and did a term paper on Julius Caesar that got him an A+ in his Latin class. In the middle of January he learned how to skate. Johnny had always been scared of ice-skating. He told himself that he had weak ankles and a poor sense of balance, but the truth was he was just plain afraid. Fergie told Johnny he was crazy to just stand around all winter with his hands in his pockets, watching other people have fun. So as soon as Round Pond was solidly frozen over, Fergie dragged Johnny down there and taught him to skate. It wasn't easy. Johnny fell down a lot at first, and sometimes when he came limping home after a skating session, his body felt like one big bruise. Gradually, though, he learned to keep his balance, and after two weeks he was flying along the ice, to the delight and amazement of Fergie and the professor. The professor was an old skating buff, and he started kidding Johnny and challenging him to races. After going skating, the three of them would always wind up by the fireplace in the professor's house, and they would drink mulled cider and sing old football songs and tell jokes and roast marshmallows over the fire.

The winter rolled past, and spring came. One Saturday afternoon early in April, Johnny and Fergie took a hike around the chain of ponds at the eastern end of Duston Heights. The two of them tramped for hours, laughing and singing and trading wisecracks. Around six in the evening, when the sun was setting, Johnny and Fergie stopped at the top of a hill to stare at the view. The reddish sunlight stained the ripply water of Spy Pond below them. On the far bank stood the old brick pumping station, with its green copper turrets. Its windows had turned to blobs of golden fire.

"Wow!" said Fergie as he looked all around with his hands on his hips. "It looks great from up here, doesn't it?"

Johnny said nothing. They had been hiking for a long time, and he was a little out of breath. His face was red and he felt faint. "Yeah, it's nice," he said at last, in a weak, throaty voice. "But I'm starved, an' I feel kind of dizzy. What's the shortest way home?"

Fergie laughed. "Aw, c'mon, Dixon!" he said in a jeering voice. "What're you gonna do when they getcha in the army? You'll hafta hike twenty-five miles every morning before breakfast, an' then after that . . ."

Fergie's voice trailed away. He had been talking with his back to Johnny, but he turned when he heard a thud. It was the sound of a body falling. Horrified, Fergie looked down and he saw his friend lying in a heap on the trail.

CHAPTER FIVE

In an instant Fergie was on his knees. He rolled Johnny over and began fumbling madly with the zipper on Johnny's Windbreaker. His mind ran through all the Boy Scout first-aid things you were supposed to do for an unconscious person: loosen the clothing around his neck, make sure he hasn't swallowed his tongue . . . Fergie did all the things he could remember, but he still felt panicky. Johnny was breathing, but his breath was coming in little gasps, and his eyes were closed. What was wrong with him?

"Help! Hey, help, somebody!" Fergie yelled, cupping his hands around his mouth.

There was no response. Scrambling to his feet again, Fergie ran down the trail, bellowing at the top of his voice. In the gathering darkness he tripped over rocks and almost fell, but he kept careening on until he had almost reached the bottom of the wooded hill. As he rounded a turn, he suddenly ran slam-bang into a hiker. He was a bald, middle-aged man who had been strolling through the woods. He had heard Fergie's yells, and he had started up the hill when Fergie came cannoning into him. As soon as they had both recovered a bit, Fergie began babbling about his friend and he tugged violently at the man's arm.

"Easy, easy, young fella!" said the man as he fought to free his arm from Fergie's grip. "I'm coming, I'm coming, don't worry!"

Back up the hill the two of them went. As soon as the man saw Johnny, he ordered Fergie to go get an ambulance as fast as he could. Fergie tore down the hill again and out toward Emerson Street, which ran past the park where the ponds were. When he got there, Fergie flagged down a car, and he was taken to a phone booth so he could call the hospital. Soon the eerie wail of the ambulance's siren could be heard, and Fergie saw the flashing red light moving down the street. Help was on the way—but was it going to be in time?

Later that same night, Johnny lay in a bed in Hannah Duston Hospital. He was pale and still, his eyes were closed, and his hands lay limply on the green blanket. Once more the livid red marks were on his nose and his neck. Once more his mouth was twisted into a hateful sneer. But this time Johnny was much sicker, much closer to death. He was having a lot of trouble breathing, and his pulse was extremely faint. Johnny had been in an oxygen tent for a while, but now the plastic sheeting lay folded back and Doc Schermerhorn stood over him. Nearby, tensely watching the doctor, stood Professor Childermass. He was biting his lip and toying nervously with the Phi Beta Kappa key on his watch chain. In an armchair in the corner sat Gramma Dixon. She was busily knitting, with lowered eyes. She looked up at Johnny often, frowned, and then went back to her knitting.

"How is he, doctor?" asked the professor in a low, tense voice.

"He's not good," Doc Schermerhorn muttered as he lifted Johnny's right eyelid and shone the light of his little black-hooded lamp into the eye. "He's in a coma, an' for the life o' me I can't figure out why. There's no reason. . . ."

No reason, indeed! growled the professor to himself. As he stood there watching the doctor, the professor had to fight down the urge to give him a piece of his mind. Was the old fool so dense that he couldn't see what had happened? The ghost of Warren Windrow had come back again, to take possession of Johnny's body. All the signs were there—couldn't he see that? Then the professor reminded himself that doctors did not believe in black magic or demonic possession. There was no point in trying to convince Doc Schermerhorn—or any other doctor—that the powers of darkness were at work. They would all just have to stand by, helplessly, as the ghost slowly choked the life out of Johnny. The more he thought, the angrier and more frustrated the professor got, and finally he realized that he couldn't stay there any longer. Abruptly, he turned on his heel and walked out. He marched down the hall to a small smoking lounge and pulled a pack of cigarettes out of his pocket. After fumbling a bit, he managed to light one, and then he began to pace furiously up and down.

"It won't happen, it can't happen, I won't LET it happen!" growled the professor as he paced back and forth, spewing smelly smoke into the air. But he knew, deep down in his heart, that there was a good chance the horrible ghost would win this time. A very good chance. Gloom descended on the professor and he could feel a spell of weepiness coming on. Angrily, he stubbed out his cigarette in an ashtray and headed for the elevator.

When the professor unlocked the front door of his house and stepped inside, it occurred to him that he had never seen the old place looking quite so dismal and empty. He remembered all the chess games and happy conversations he had had with Johnny. He thought about the chocolate cakes that Johnny had helped him bake— and eat.

"Blast it all anyway!" roared the professor, and he threw his key ring against the wall and watched it bounce back onto the middle of the hall rug.

The phone began to ring.

It's probably some blubberbrain asking for contributions to something, thought the professor as he picked up the key ring and put it on the shelf in front of the mirror. He had half a mind not to answer the phone, but he could never resist a ringing phone, so he stalked into the dining room and picked up the receiver.

"Hello!" he said grumpily. "Whoever it is, keep it short, because I'm *very* tired and want to go to bed!"

"Good heavens!" exclaimed the voice at the other end. "Do you always answer your phone that way? It's no wonder you're a bachelor!" It was his old friend, Professor Coote.

"Oh, it's *you*, Charley!" exclaimed the professor, feeling suddenly very ashamed of himself. "Look, I'm sorry to sound so snappish, but it's been a thoroughly rotten evening, and I'm bushed. Something awful has happened."

As calmly as he could, the professor explained what had happened to Johnny. He tried to sound optimistic, but he didn't pull any punches: Johnny's life was hanging by a thread, and it was only his powerful will to live that was keeping the worst from happening.

After the professor had finished, there was a shocked silence at the other end of the line. Finally Professor Coote found his voice.

"Lord above!" he said mournfully. "We were afraid that something like this would happen, but . . . The poor kid! Roderick, I may have a ray of hope for us."

"It's about time a ray of hope arrived," said the professor. "I'll take a nice shiny one, with gilt edges, if you don't mind. Have you found out something about the sinister Windrow family?"

"I have indeed!" said Professor Coote excitedly. "I have turned up some very peculiar clues that may lead us to a pair of magic amulets that have been lost for many centuries. And these talismans could help us in our battle against the spirit of Warren Windrow."

"Well, come on, Charley!" snapped Professor Childermass impatiently. "Tell me what you've found out!"

With a lot of hemming and hawing, Professor Coote began to tell his tale. He had done a lot of reading and he had found out about an old man named Zebulon Windrow. Zebulon had gotten rich in the lumber business back in the 1880s, and he had built a mansion and an enormous church on a hilltop estate overlooking the Hudson River, not far from Haverstraw, New York. The church at the estate was an exact replica of Salisbury Cathedral in England, and it had a four-hundred-foot-high steeple. In the crypt under the church a lot of the Windrows were buried, and in one tomb was the body of a man who had married Zebulon Windrow's only daughter, in 1898. The man's name was Edmund French, and he had been an ensign in the United States Navy. On his tomb a very strange inscription had been carved: *Ensign French Is the Boss.* The inscription had been put there by Zebulon, who outlived his son-in-law.

"Now, isn't that a peculiar thing to put on somebody's tomb?" asked Professor Coote. "And I'll tell you something else that's even more bizarre: Ensign French had his name changed before he died. Instead of being Edmund French, he became Ulysses Theodore French. Now—"

"Charley, I don't mean to spoil your fun," said Professor Childermass acidly, "but will you *please* tell me where all this is leading to?"

"I'm getting to it, Roderick—please try to be patient. It's the initials U.T. that are important, and I'll tell you why in a minute. I read a history of the Windrow family and in it I noticed a lot of people with the initials U.T.: Ulrica Tadcaster Windrow, Uther Tench Windrow, and so on. Well, do you know what I think? I think that somehow the Windrows managed to get hold of the Urim and the Thummim."

Professor Childermass was astounded. He knew a lot of history, and he knew that these two things were two enchanted objects that had belonged to the ancient Israelites. According to the Bible, the Urim and the Thummim hung on the breastplate that the High Priest of the Levites wore. No one knew what the Urim and the Thummim looked like, but they were supposed to be like crystal balls that had let the Israelites know what God wanted them to do.

"The Urim and the Thummim!" exclaimed Professor Childermass. "But they must have vanished centuries ago, along with the Ark of the Covenant. How could—"

"I don't know how the Windrows got hold of them," said his friend calmly. "But the Urim and the Thummim would explain how there got to be so many wizards and witches in the Windrow family. I could be wrong, of course, but . . . well, would you care to hear the rest of my story?"

"Go on!" sighed Professor Childermass. "You're the one who's paying the long-distance bill!"

"All righty!" said Professor Coote enthusiastically. "I think that the Urim and the Thummim may be out at that estate on the Hudson River. After all, it's old Zebulon's estate, and he was the richest and most powerful member of the whole creepy family. And it seems to me that the logical place to look would be in Ensign French's tomb. In the first place there's that odd phrase, *Ensign French Is the Boss.* According to the guidebook that I read, that phrase is carved in various places on walls all over the estate. And there's another weird phrase that shows up: *Ensign French Is the Unfortunate Traveler.* That phrase is in a stained-glass window in the library of Zebulon's mansion. Unfortunate Traveler, U.T.—get it? So, as I said, I think those two magic trinkets may just be in the tomb of this French character. I mean, doesn't it seem reasonable to you?"

Professor Childermass groaned. "Charley, I honestly don't know what's reasonable at this hour of the night. I have a headache, and I'm dead tired. But if there's a chance—any chance at all—of finding something that will save Johnny, I'd turn the whole Hudson Valley upside down! Tell me, what do you think my chances are of getting inside this estate to poke around and play burglar?"

"I'd say your chances are pretty good," his friend replied. "The Windrow Estate stood empty for years after Zebulon died, and the whole place started falling into ruins. Not so long ago a private foundation bought the place, and they're fixing it up so it can be opened as a tourist attraction this Memorial Day. During the daytime there'll probably be an army of workmen at the estate, but if you sneak in in the evening, you'll probably have the place to yourself. I'd help you, but I scare easily, and I have bad legs. I'd just be in your way."

"I'm sure you would be," said Professor Childermass with a chuckle. "But look, Charley—my head is throbbing and I'm asleep on my feet. Tomorrow I'll start making plans to go to the estate. But before I hang up, I have one little question to ask: You say that you scare easily. What do you think there'll be at the Windrow estate to be scared of?"

"Who knows, Roderick? Who on earth knows?" And with that, Professor Coote hung up.

CHAPTER SIX

The next morning, when he woke up, Professor Childermass could hardly believe that he had had that strange telephone conversation with his old friend. Now that his head was clear, he wondered if he really ought to go off on this wild goose chase. Could the Urim and the Thummim really be at that old estate? It seemed very unlikely, but on the other hand, the thing that had happened to Johnny was pretty unlikely. And how else could he be saved? The doctors at the hospital couldn't drive the spirit of Warren Windrow out of Johnny's body. A long shot was better than no shot at all. So the professor made his mind up: He would go. For days he planned. He ransacked his basement for tools, and he dug an old leather satchel out of his attic. He drove up to Durham and got a guidebook and a map from Professor Coote—these had been issued by the foundation that was fixing up the Windrow estate. The next evening the professor called up Fergie and asked him to come over to his house. No, he wouldn't say over the phone what he wanted him for, but he claimed that it was very important. It was about a plan he had, to save Johnny's life.

When Fergie arrived at the professor's house, the old man marched him into the living room, gave him a piece of chocolate cake and a fork, and started telling him his plan. He explained about the Urim and the Thummim, Ensign French, the tomb with the weird inscription, and old Zebulon. Fergie sat listening in openmouthed amazement. He even forgot to eat his cake.

". . . and so that's what I think we ought to do," said the professor, finishing up. "I want you to come along and help me. I need someone who's gutsy and resourceful. I need someone who won't cave in when the going gets rough—and that's you, my friend. You know what's happened to Johnny, and you also know that there's very little chance of saving him unless we fight magic with magic. Will you go with me to find the Urim and the Thummim?"

Fergie put his uneaten cake down on the coffee table and pondered. There was a doubtful frown on his face. He had seen Johnny's twisted face; he had seen and heard a lot of strange things in the last few months. But he was a skeptical kid, and he didn't really want to believe that an evil spirit had taken possession of Johnny's body. There might be some other explanation, a scientific one.

"I . . . I dunno, professor," said Fergie slowly. "All this stuff about amulets and devils sounds kinda nutty to me. Maybe Johnny really does have a brain sickness, like the doctors say."

The professor was beginning to get exasperated. "Oh, brain sickness, your grandmother!" he growled. "You told me that he saw a box of matches in the ice cream parlor and called them *loco focos*. Well, I looked up that weird little phrase and it's what they called matches back in the 1830s. How the dickens would Johnny have known about that, unless he was possessed by the spirit of somebody who was alive in the 1830s?"

"He might've looked it up, same's you did," said Fergie calmly.

The professor ground his teeth and glared at Fergie. Then, without a word, he walked over to the sideboard and jerked a drawer open. After fumbling a bit, he pulled out a paper-wrapped parcel and a magnifying glass. With a snort he dashed back to the coffee table and laid these things down in front of Fergie. As Fergie stared with a puzzled expression, he unwrapped the parcel and laid the magnifying glass down next to it.

"All right!" said the professor fiercely. "You want to be logical, let's be logical! There are the glass photograph and the gold coin—you've seen them before, I know, but I have a few things to tell you that may surprise you. Pick up the magnifying glass and have a look at the buttons on the coat that the man in the photograph is wearing. Have a good look."

Fergie took the magnifying glass in his hand and peered. His eyes opened wide, and he leaned a little closer and peered some more. "The buttons say W.W.," he said quietly. "So it must be a picture of—"

"Warren Windrow," snapped the professor, cutting him off. "Of course, it *could* be a photo of a young man named Woodrow Wallace or Walter Wintergreen, but I don't think that's terribly likely. All right, let's talk about the gold coin. I looked it up, and it was minted by somebody named J. S. Ormsby, in Sacramento, California, in the year 1849. And that coin is so rare, there is only *one* of them around! How the blue blazes did Johnny get his hands on one? And why was he keeping it in his bureau drawer, along with a photo that is a hundred years old? Can you come up with any logical explanations?"

Fergie shook his head.

"All right then!" the professor said, stabbing his finger at Fergie. "Will you come and help me before it's too late?"

Fergie turned pale, and he nodded. In a low voice, he said that he would do what he could to save Johnny.

The next day Professor Childermass called up Fergie's mother and he did some fast talking. He told her that he wanted to take Fergie on a short trip to the Hudson River Valley to see Washington Irving's home and other places of interest. To make the trip sound reasonable, he said that it would help Fergie in his schoolwork, and he added that Fergie needed to get away from Duston Heights for a while, so that he would stop thinking about Johnny and his tragic illness. Fergie would have to be ready to go early Friday morning, so of course he'd have to be excused from school for that day. Was this possible? At first Mrs. Ferguson resisted, but the professor could be very charming and persuasive when he wanted to be, and at last she gave in. She would get her son excused, and she hoped that he would have a wonderful time.

On the very next Friday morning, at a quarter past ten, Fergie was sitting at the kitchen table in his home, waiting for the phone to ring. He was wearing his motorcycle outfit: skintight blue jeans, black ankle-high boots, and a black-leather jacket covered with chrome-plated studs and red-glass reflectors. Near him, on the worn linoleum, stood his suitcase. It was old and beat-up, and had dirty red-plaid sides and a zipper. Into it he had stuffed everything he thought he would need, including a large red portable searchlight and a small crowbar that he had swiped from his dad's tool chest in the basement. His dad wouldn't miss the crowbar right away—he was off on one of his weekend selling trips. Mr. Ferguson sold encyclopedias, Bibles, and mail-order shoes, and he didn't make a lot of money. But he worked like a beaver driving around the countryside in his old blue Ford, trying to drum up more business. Fergie worried about his dad; he was afraid that he was working too hard. Fergie thought about the Urim and the Thummim, the magical doojiggers that he and the professor were going after. After they saved Johnny from the evil spirit, perhaps they could sell the amulets to a museum for a lot of money. He hoped so. . . .

Fergie winced. He felt guilty to be thinking about money at a time like this, with Johnny lying sick in bed. But when he looked around at the shabby furnishings of the living room, he thought about how nice it would be to come waltzing in the door and throw a big bundle of hundred-dollar bills on the table. It wouldn't be just nice, it would be like heaven!

"Fergie? Wasn't the professor going to call you a half hour ago? What do you suppose he's doing?" This was Mrs. Ferguson, calling through the open kitchen doorway. She was a worn-looking, mild little woman with stringy gray hair. She had been doing the dishes and had been having some second thoughts about this trip that her son was taking. She knew the professor, and she trusted him in spite of his being nervous, irritable, and a bit on the eccentric side. Still, she wouldn't have been terribly surprised to have him phone and call the trip off. She would even have been a bit relieved if that had happened.

"I dunno why he hasn't called, Mom," said Fergie, answering his mother's question. "He told me to be ready at a quarter to ten, an' he said he'd give me a buzz before he came over. He's usually so darned persnickety about stuff like that. . . ."

The phone rang.

In an instant Fergie was on his feet. He ran to the sideboard and ripped the receiver from the cradle. It was the professor. In his usual raspy voice he apologized for being late and said that he'd be over in ten minutes. Fergie hung up and heaved a big sigh of relief. He had been kind of uncertain about this trip at first, but now he was all worked up and ready to go.

Exactly ten minutes later Professor Childermass pulled up in front of the Fergusons' house in his mud-spattered maroon Pontiac. Fergie was waiting on the porch with his suitcase in his hand. His mother was right beside him, and now she gave him a big smooch on the cheek. Fergie winced—it always embarrassed him when his mother kissed him in public.

"Have a good time!" she called as he took off, running down the walk. "Did you remember to pack your baby Brownie camera?"

"Yeah, Mom, I did!" Fergie called back. This was a lie. He hated to fool with cameras, but his mother thought they were an essential part of any sightseeing trip. Oh, well—he could apologize to her when he got back.

Slam. Into the trunk went Fergie's suitcase. Fergie climbed into the front seat, the professor revved up the engine, and they went peeling off in a cloud of exhaust smoke. The trip was on. They drove for hours across Massachusetts and through a corner of Connecticut. The professor drove fast—though not as fast as he usually did. Around two-thirty in the afternoon they reached the Bear Mountain bridge on the Hudson River. Beyond it, in both directions, high hills and riverside cliffs stretched away into blue distances. As they drove across the bridge, the professor told Fergie stories about the Dutch settlers who had lived there long ago. He also pointed out that they were leaving Washington Irving's estate behind. Fergie knew they weren't really on a sightseeing trip. They were here to dig in the grave of the long-dead, mysterious Ensign French to find the two ancient talismans that would bring Johnny out of his coma.

"Hey, prof!" said Fergie, as they swerved north on a road that led away from the bridge. "Are we very far from the estate?"

The professor lit a black-and-gold cigarette and blew out a long, thin stream of smoke. "No," he said with a confident smile, "we're not far from the place at all. If we follow this road for a while, we wind up in a little bitty town called Van Twiller, and the entrance to the Windrow estate is only a mile or so outside the town. We are not going straight to the estate. At this time of day the place will be swarming with workmen, so we will just have to wait. Tomorrow night will be the time to make our move, I think. In the meantime, we are going to get ourselves a place to stay in lovely little Van

Twiller, and then we are going to pretend to be tourists and prive out past the place to case the joint before we knock it over." The professor chuckled wickedly. "*Case the joint. Knock it over*," he said quietly, savoring the phrases he had used. "My, my! I'm beginning to sound like a gangster in a movie! As a matter of fact, I'm beginning to feel like one too. . . . Heavens! What would my dear sainted mother have said?" With a quick flick of his wrist, he threw the stub of his cigarette out the vent window, and he began to whistle jauntily through his teeth. There was a rakish, devil-may-care air about him as he drove on, and Fergie began to glance at him skeptically. He was wondering what kind of trouble this crazy old man was going to land the two of them in.

The road wound among steep, rugged hills. Once, from the top of a rise, they saw a tall stone steeple glowing in the afternoon light, and they began to get excited because they knew that the estate must be nearby. Then the road sank into a deep valley, and the steeple vanished. It was close to three-thirty when they drove into Van Twiller. The downtown part of the town was just a collection of old red-brick buildings grouped around a grassy town square. In the center of the square, on a low pedestal, stood a statue of a fireman and a brown sandstone drinking fountain. Pigeons were strutting in the grass, and people were reading newspapers on benches. As the maroon Pontiac rolled into the square, a hoarse bell in a church steeple clanged once.

"Ah, small-town America!" sighed the professor. "I

keep thinking I might want to retire to some place like this, even though I know that I would go buggy if I had to stay here more than a couple of days. Does the guidebook say how many people live here?"

Fergie flipped the pages of the small blue book he was holding. "Hmm ... lemme see ... it says pop. 500. Pretty small. Where're we gonna stay?"

"Wait'll you see," said the professor, chuckling. "You'll probably hate it."

The car pulled into a parking space in front of a four-story brick building with a fancy greenish copper cornice. Over the door was a wooden sign that said VAN TWILLER HOTEL.

"Is *this* it?" groaned Fergie. "I thought we were gonna stay in a motel!"

"Well, you thought wrong," snapped the professor. "Motels are for people who are fleeing from the police—they are not for respectable folk like you and me. Now quit grousing and help me bring the bags inside. After we check in, we can go down the street and eat. I saw Somebody-or-Other's Steak House on the way in, and those places usually have pretty good burgers. Come on!"

A few minutes later Fergie was following the professor into the cool, musty-smelling lobby of the old hotel. In one corner was a high, marble-topped desk with pigeonholes behind it for mail and a rack full of room keys. A grumpy-looking old man in a navy-blue suit smiled at the professor and then glowered at Fergie.

"Will you be wanting a room, sir?" he asked in a voice that was full of weariness.

"I have one reserved, I hope," said the professor crisply, as he set his suitcase down. "My name is—"

"Wait . . . there it is, I've got it," said the man, pressing the page with a knobbly finger. "Professor Simcox, reserved for two nights. Very good. We can put you in—"

"That's *Childermass*," said the professor, pronouncing the name with extreme care. "C-h-i-l-d-e—"

"Right you are," said the man, giving him a bored look over the top of his glasses. "You'll be in Room two-thirteen, Mr. Chimcark." And as the professor glared furiously, the man turned away, fetched down the key from the board, and laid it on the desk. Fergie had a hard time keeping a straight face, but somehow he managed. Biting his lip, he picked up his suitcase and followed the professor across the lobby toward the flight of red-carpeted stairs.

Their hotel room turned out to be quite nice. A wine-colored carpet covered the floor, and there was an oval marble-topped table by the windows. Side by side on the rug stood twin brass bedsteads topped with shiny knobs, and a hurricane lamp with a delicate rose-red globe cast its warm, friendly light over the scarred black night table. The professor was delighted with the old-time quality of the furnishings, but they made Fergie a bit nervous. He remembered the way the desk clerk had glared at him, and he felt sure that if he broke anything, his family would wind up having to pay for it.

After they had gotten washed up, the two travelers went across the square to Steve's Steak House and stuffed themselves on cheeseburgers and french fries. Fergie had a Coke, and the professor drank coffee, and both finished up with homemade blueberry pie à la mode. When they were done, the two travelers felt full and at peace with the world. However, they had not forgotten what they had come all this way for. When they sauntered out into the square again, they were glad to see that it was still light outside. Fergie squinted up at the sun, which hovered over a mass of trees in the distance.

"Hey, professor," he said hesitantly, "d'ya think we oughta go out an' have a look at that . . . whatchama-callit estate now?"

The professor took out his watch and squinted at it. It was a little after five. "Yes, I suppose that is what we ought to do," he said as he snapped the gold-plated lid shut and jammed the watch back into his vest pocket. "By the way," he added, "you don't sound like your usual overeager self. Are you afraid we'll get tossed in the clink for trespassing?"

Fergie gave the professor a dirty look. "If you're not scared, I'm not scared either," he muttered sullenly. "Come on—let's go!"

The professor grinned. "Stout fellow!" he said, patting Fergie on the shoulder. "For the time being, however, you can relax—we're not going to pull anything fancy this evening. I just want to see what the place looks like."

Fergie and the professor walked quickly across the square, got into the car, and drove off. Once they were outside the town, they followed a narrow two-lane blacktop out to the Windrow estate. Long before they got there, they could see the tall stone steeple rising over the trees. One side of it glowed reddish-orange in the light of the late afternoon sun, and birds were wheeling around the bases of the pinnacles. The professor and Fergie were driving along next to the red sandstone wall that surrounded the grounds of the estate. The enormous church loomed very near, shadowy and somehow threatening, like a crouching monster of stone. Next to the church was the mansion, a grim square block with a large, egg-shaped copper dome rising up out of the middle. Atop the dome was a funny little doodad shaped like a saltshaker, and from it sprouted a short pole with a metal flag on it. The letter W had been cut out of the metal and could be seen glowing sky blue against the dark background.

Slowly the car rolled along, in the shadow of the grimy red wall. Ahead, Fergie and the professor saw a gateway. Two tall red-granite pillars rose above the level of the wall, and atop each one was a weathered and pitted stone skull. Between the pillars large black iron gates could be seen, and as the car drew close to them, the travelers could see that they were chained shut.

The professor's car slowed to a crawl and then pulled

off onto a sandy piece of ground that was directly across from the gates. Beyond the iron bars Fergie and the professor could see a panel truck parked on the gravel drive that led to the front door of the mansion. Near it was a cement mixer, and beyond they could see some scaffolding that had been thrown up against one wall of the church. But there were no workmen around.

"Some place, huh?" said Fergie, as he gazed up in awe at the closed gates. "How much d'ya think it cost to build a great big huge dump like this?"

The professor chuckled. "You're a typical American, Byron—you're fascinated by how much things cost. Well, take a good look at the expensive old heap of stones. This is the place we're going to have to break into. Think it'll be a pushover?"

Fergie grinned confidently. "Sure, prof! No problem at all. We just scoot on out there tomorrow night with a ladder, climb that wall, an'—bingo! We're in! Or we could . . ." Fergie's voice trailed away, and a gleam appeared in his eyes. "Hey, prof!" he said suddenly. "Why don't we go over and see if we can get in right now?"

The professor was startled by this suggestion. He thought a second or two, and then he laughed. "Oh, not *now*, Byron!" he exclaimed. "I'm dressed in my good clothes, and on top of everything else, I'm tired. Let's wait till tomorrow night."

Fergie gave the professor a scornful look. "Aw, come on, prof!" he said in a taunting voice. "Are you scared to go over there now an' see if we can get in?"

The professor did not like to be kidded. He scowled at Fergie. "Now see here, Byron," he began, "I am not a coward. Who planned this trip, anyway? Whose idea was it to break into the estate, my fine feathered friend?"

Fergie shrugged. "Okay, okay, so you planned the big wonderful expedition! Then why don't you wanta go over there an' rattle a couple of doors? Huh?"

The professor spluttered a bit, and when he finally managed to calm down, he answered.

"Oh, very *well*!" he said irritably. "Let us wait half an hour to see if anyone comes out of that gate. Then we will trot over there and see if there's some way of getting in. Will that make you happy?"

Fergie nodded and grinned. They waited. The sun had set and it was getting dark. A night wind sprang up, and an owl began to hoot in the woods nearby. After a half-hour had passed, the professor went to the trunk of his car, opened it, and took out two nickel-plated flashlights. He gave one to Fergie and took one himself. As they started toward the gate, they noticed something that had been hidden by a clump of juniper trees that grew near the road. It was a small stone gatehouse that was built into the wall near the main gate. It had only one window, which was blocked up with bricks, but there was a narrow green door set in a round-topped arch.

"Hey, look!" Fergie exclaimed. "It's a door! See, what'd I tell ya?"

The professor laughed. "Yes, it's a door, isn't it? And

I'll bet it's locked and backed with a piece of sheet steel an inch thick. But I suppose you won't be happy till you've rattled it, will you?"

Fergie stepped boldly forward through the tall, swishy grass. The professor followed, muttering unpleasantly to himself, and soon the two were standing in front of the weathered door. Fergie pointed the beam of his flashlight at the knob. Then he said, "Here goes nothin'!" and grasped the knob firmly. He twisted it and pushed, hard. With a dull rattle and a scraping sound, the door moved inward.

CHAPTER SEVEN

In silence, Fergie and the professor stared at the half-open door. For some reason neither one of them wanted to take the first step forward. Finally, Fergie summoned up his courage. "Hey, how about that!" he said in a voice that was a little too loud. "It's not locked!"

The professor said nothing. To his logical mind this open door did not make any sense. Why chain up the main gate and leave this door open? But then he thought of something.

"It may be a little too early to celebrate, Byron," he said as he stepped forward. "I mean, we may not be able to get any farther than this stupid gatehouse. Let's have a look."

With the flashlight beam moving across the floor in front of him, the professor stepped into the tiny room. Then he saw the other door. It hung halfway open. Beyond, they could see a gravel driveway and the looming shape of the mansion.

"Well, I *never!*" muttered the professor as he stepped through the doorway. "If I were the owner of this place, I would fire the people who are in charge of locking up at night. Let's just have a brief little stroll around and then go back to the hotel for the night. Okay?"

Fergie nodded, and he followed the professor down the gravel drive toward the mansion. It was twilight now, and they could not see much without their flashlights. Slowly they moved forward, and the only sound was the crunching of their shoes on the gravel. As Fergie walked along, an odd thought popped into his head: *Somebody left the door open on purpose. Somebody wanted us to come in.* This was a silly thought, and normally it would have made Fergie laugh. But he didn't laugh. Instead, he glanced nervously at the vast, shadowy church. What if a figure stepped out of the dark and moved toward them? What would they do? It was not a pleasant thought, and Fergie tried hard to put it out of his mind.

Suddenly the professor stopped, and he reached out and grabbed Fergie by the arm. "My friend," he said quietly, "I do not want to go poking around in that mansion tonight, even if all the doors are wide open.

And I certainly do not want to fool around in the church without any tools. So let's just mosey around to the backyard of the estate. Maybe we can peer over the wall and see the beautiful Hudson River shining in the moonlight. We'll just have a quick peek, call it an evening, and go back to the hotel."

Fergie followed the professor around the side of the mansion. Quickly they padded across the long, matted grass and dodged a wheelbarrow that had been left by the workmen. They were on the back lawn. In the distance they could see the wall that surrounded the estate, and off to the right was a small grove of trees. Rising over the trees was the dome of some kind of small building. It was made of white stone, and glimmered faint and ghostly in the light of the moon, which had just risen over the roof of the church.

Fergie stared. "What is that thing over there?" he asked.

The professor squinted into the darkness. "Oh, you mean the dome? That is probably what they call a folly. In the old days they put up weird little buildings on the grounds of estates, just to make everything look pretty. Shall we give it the once-over?"

Fergie agreed, and they trotted off toward the grove of trees. A flagstone walk wound among the dark trunks, and it led to a flight of marble steps. The door of the building was made of bronze, and it was flanked by fluted columns. Over the door was an oblong slab, with the words TEMPLE OF THE INNER LIGHT chiseled on it. The place looked utterly deserted. The marble pillars were grimy, and pine needles littered the steps. A sagging cobweb hung across one corner of the doorway.

"Fancy, eh?" said the professor as he played the beam of his light over the front of the temple. "I wonder if old Zeb had garden parties out . . ."

Suddenly the professor stopped talking. He was staring at a statue that stood in a niche on the front of the temple. It was a statue of a short, hunched figure in a monk's robe. The hood of the robe was large, and hung down over the creature's face, but you could see something dangling from one long, drooping sleeve. It looked like an octopus's tentacle. Below the statue was an inscription: *To him are given the keys of the Bottomless Pit.*

Fergie let out a long, low whistle. "Boy!" he said, shaking his head. "They coulda had some great Halloween parties out here with a thing like that around!"

The professor grimaced. "I don't think you would have enjoyed the parties that good old Zeb gave," he said. "Witches' Sabbaths would have been right up his alley, wouldn't they? Euchh! This thing is giving me the creeps! What d'ye say we . . ."

The professor froze. He had heard something—a loud crackling, crunching noise. It seemed to be coming from somewhere beside the dark, gloomy temple. As he and Fergie stood dead still, listening, the crunching went on. Then, suddenly, the air was filled with the sound of barking.

"Hey!" Fergie exclaimed. "It's just a dog! I wonder what he's doin' around here."

The professor sighed. "I'm sure I don't know, but I will say I am very relieved to find that it is only . . ."

Again the professor's voice died. The dog had stopped barking, but it started whining and whimpering in a pitiful, frightened way. A long, anguished howl filled the air, and then it was cut short.

Fergie and the professor stood motionless, listening for more noises—but none came. When the professor finally spoke, he sounded tense and frightened.

"Byron," he said in a low voice, "it may be a foolish thing to do, but I want to go around behind the temple and find out what has happened to that dog. Are you with me?"

Fergie wanted to say, *You're right, pal, it is a dumb thing to do!* But he merely nodded and followed the professor into the wet, dripping shrubbery that grew close to the temple. Carefully they inched their way along, following the curving marble wall. Finally they came out into a small clearing at the rear of the temple. At first they saw nothing. The two flashlight beams moved over the matted grass, and then they stopped on the same spot.

"Oh, my God!" gasped the professor. "Lord have mercy on us!"

They both stared, and felt their blood run cold. Lying on the grass was the body of a small collie dog. It was dead. There was not much doubt about that. All the flesh had been sucked away from the dog's head, leaving only a bleached white skull.

Fergie swallowed hard and closed his eyes. When he opened them, the fearful shape was still there. He turned to the professor, but the old man said nothing; he merely took Fergie by the arm and led him back around to the front of the temple. In silence they walked along the winding flagstone path and then onto the moonlit grass again. They went out through the little gatehouse and crossed the road. Finally, when they were standing by the car again, Fergie spoke.

"We shoulda buried the poor thing," he said sadly.

"Yes," added the professor. "We should have, I suppose. But I wanted to get out of that place as quickly as possible. I can't imagine who—or what—could have done such a thing, but I will tell you this: I have a plastic bottle of holy water in my glove compartment, and when we come back here, I'm going to be carrying it with me. I wish I had the little silver crucifix that Father Higgins gave to Johnny, but it seems to have disappeared. Mrs. Dixon searched in Johnny's room, but she couldn't find it."

"Do you think it would help?" asked Fergie skeptically. "I mean, it might just've been some crazy maniac who killed that dog."

"And left it in that condition, and did it that fast?" said the professor with a grimace. "I doubt it. Even maniacs need time to do their work. Come on. Let's get in the car and go back to the hotel. I've had enough of this rotten place for one night."

CHAPTER EIGHT

When Fergie got up the next day, he looked out the window of the hotel room and he groaned. The sky was gray, and it was raining. He knew that they were going to have to wait until evening to try their second break-in, and it looked as if they were going to spend the whole time cooped up in their room. The professor was more cheerful, however: He had lived in England, so he was used to rotten weather. After they dressed and washed up, the professor dug his collapsible umbrella out of the suitcase and took Fergie across the street to Steve's Steak House for breakfast. They pored over the map and the guidebook while they ate, and went back to their room and played chess for a while. Neither of them had gotten much sleep the night before, so late in the afternoon they took a nap.

When they awoke, the rain had stopped and it was colder. As the sun moved downward, fog came rolling up the Hudson and drifted into the town. Fergie and the professor paced about in their hotel room for a while, fussed, and grumbled about the weather. Around a quarter past six, the professor changed into his prowling-around clothes: a gray sweat shirt, grass-stained khaki trousers, and tennis shoes. There was a large baggy pocket on the front of the sweat shirt, and into it the professor put the holy water bottle. Fergie put on blue jeans and a plaid shirt, and he dug the red searchlight out of his suitcase. Meanwhile, the professor checked the two old nickel-plated flashlights that he normally carried in the car, and the "burglar" equipment in the leather satchel. One by one he laid the items out on the bed: a hammer and chisel, a coil of rope, a small pair of binoculars, a screwdriver, three files, a jackknife, a mallet, and a brace and auger for boring holes. To this collection he added Fergie's crowbar; he replaced everything in the satchel, and finally, at a quarter to seven, the two of them went downstairs, got into the car, and drove off toward the Windrow estate.

When Fergie and the professor pulled up across from the main entrance of the estate, they saw that the church and the mansion were wrapped in swirling gray fog. Overhead, the stone steeple rose into the dark sky, and at its very tip a red warning light glowed. Two white globe lights burned by the main gate, and haloes of mist hung around them.

"Wow!" said Fergie as he glanced out the car window. "This looks like a Sherlock Holmes movie, doesn't it?"

"Please keep your jokes to yourself," growled the professor as he got out of the car. "We have a job to do, and it's not likely to be terribly pleasant. You can yuk it up when we're back in our hotel room, safe and sound. Okay? Let's go."

The professor got the tool satchel out of the trunk, and he snapped on one of his small flashlights. With Fergie by his side, he trotted quickly across the road. When they got to the gatehouse, they found that the wooden door was still unlocked. Once again, as they pushed their way in, Fergie felt a pang of real fear: What if the creature that had killed the dog was waiting for them? It was better not to think that way, though, and Fergie forced himself to smile bravely as he stepped through the dark gatehouse and out onto the wet gravel of the driveway.

Dead silence hung about the two explorers as they padded forward through the fog. The white beam of the searchlight stabbed out, but not very far: Always, a pale wall of mist hung beyond the light.

"Byron?" the professor rasped. "Do you have any idea of where we are? This fog is awful! It's like walking around inside a box full of cotton batting!"

Fergie waved the beam of his searchlight around. Up ahead the dark shape of a building loomed, like a cliff in a mist. "I think the church is up that way," he said uncertainly. "Anyways, it looks like it."

They plodded on, and soon they were standing in front of a flight of broad stone steps. At the top was a tall pair of bronze doors with large drum-shaped knobs.

"Oh, good night!" exclaimed the professor. "Byron, you get D minus for sense of direction. This isn't the church, it's the mansion. But as long as we're here, let's have a peek inside. There's a stained-glass window in the library, and it may have some clues that will help us. It'll only take a minute."

"Hey, come on, professor!" Fergie exclaimed as he tugged at the old man's arm. "What is this, a guided tour or somethin'? We're supposed to be over at the church, lookin' for the Urim and the Whatsis, aren't we?"

"Young man," the professor said huffily, "I know perfectly well what we're here for. But if the Urim and the Thummim aren't in the coffin, we may need to follow other clues."

Fergie shrugged and followed the professor up the steps. They paused in front of the doors, and the professor twisted one of the knobs. With a loud, dismal groan the door moved outward.

"I don't get this!" said Fergie as they stepped into the dark, cool hallway. "How come all the doors in this joint are open? Aren't they scared of burglars?"

The professor chuckled. "You're forgetting that this place is being fixed up by an army of workmen. They're traipsing in and out of these doors all day long, and at night they probably don't worry much about whether the place is completely locked up tight. They just chain the gates and kiss the place good-bye till the next morning. It's lucky for us, of course—I never was any good at lock picking. Hmm . . . I wonder where that library is. It ought to be through this door over on the right, if I remember the floor plan correctly."

Fergie quickly flashed his light down the long dark hall, and then he followed the professor. They passed a floor-polishing machine and stopped in front of a tall oak door set in a fancy carved arch. A large brass key was stuck into the door's lock, and the professor twisted it. Creaking a little, the door opened, and they stepped inside. The professor fumbled around on the wall, and his hand found an electric switch. Instantly the room was flooded with light.

"Hey!" exclaimed Fergie. "Do you think that's a smart thing to do? What if somebody drives by and sees the lights on?"

"They will think that the workmen are putting in some overtime," said the professor calmly. "Now quit griping and have a look around—we're not going to stay long."

They were in a huge, high-ceilinged room that would have reminded Fergie of his high school gym, except that built-in bookshelves stretched from floor to ceiling along three of the four walls, and a narrow balcony ran all the way around the room, so you could get at the shelves that were higher up. The shelves were empty, and tall stacks of books were standing on the floor. As he paused to run his finger over the dusty cover of a book, he heard a loud *whap!* behind him.

"Ye gods!" exclaimed the professor as he whirled around. "Don't *do* that! You nearly gave me a heart attack!"

"I didn't do it," muttered Fergie, and he turned to see what had made the noise. A book had fallen off one of the piles. Curious, Fergie ambled over and picked it up. It was a small, square book bound in watered blue silk. The gold letters on the spine said *Budge's Heraldry.* Fergie flipped the cover back, and on the flyleaf he saw a name and a date: *Zebulon Windrow July 5, 1897.*

"Hey, professor!" Fergie said loudly. "This's a book about heraldry, an' it used to belong to Zebulon Windrow—you know, the old nutcake that built this place?"

"Well, isn't that charming!" said the professor sourly. "Bring the book along, and you can read yourself to sleep with it when we get back to the hotel tonight. Come on. As you can see, there is a large window at the far end of the room, but it's as black as pitch. I had forgotten that you need sunlight or moonlight to see the details—stupid of me, eh? Let's get going."

Fergie tucked the book under his arm and moved toward the door. He watched as the professor flicked the switch and the room was plunged into darkness again. But just as they were about to turn on their flashlights, something happened. A faint glow of moonlight suddenly spread over the window, and it revealed the picture of a young man in an old-fashioned naval uniform with a double row of buttons and fringed epaulets. He had a cocked hat under his arm, and he looked very stiff and pompous. Around the picture was a wide oval border, and in the border was an inscription: ENSIGN FRENCH IS THE UNFORTUNATE TRAVELER. The picture glowed for only a few seconds, and then it went dark.

"Hmph!" said the professor as he snapped his flashlight on. "If that doesn't just beat everything! You know, Byron, while you were looking at that heraldry book, I was leafing through a couple of books on one stack. Both were copies of *The Unfortunate Traveler*, a book by an old writer named Thomas Nashe. So you see, there really is a pattern of U.T. clues leading to the Urim and the Thummim. It's not just a lot of folderol invented by Charley Coote and me."

Silently, Fergie added that U.T. might stand for *Ugly Twerp*. But he didn't argue—he turned on his light and followed the professor out the door. A stiff wind was blowing, and the fog was starting to break up. Tattered shreds of mist swirled around the church's pinnacles and tall steeple. Fergie and the professor left the driveway and padded across the wet grass toward the small stone porch that was stuck onto one side of the church. Inside the porch they found a large wooden door with a twisted ring of wrought iron hanging from it. *This one's gotta be locked!* thought Fergie, but when the professor twisted the ring to the right, a hidden latch clicked and the door swung inward. For a couple of seconds the professor paused, with his hand on the iron ring. Fergie heard him muttering, and he thought that he was saying a prayer. Then the old man gave the door a hard shove, and they went inside.

CHAPTER NINE

Fergie played the strong beam of his red searchlight around the enormous, dark church. Above them was a vaulted stone ceiling, and two rows of pointed arches marched down the nave toward the altar at the eastern end. Several tall scaffolds made of iron pipes and boards stood throughout the room. And there were whitewash buckets, bags of cement, and tool chests, signs that work had been going on. Fergie looked around in awe, but the professor was in a brisk and businesslike mood. Handing the tool bag to Fergie, he reached into his pants pocket and pulled out a dog-eared booklet—it was the guide to the Windrow estate.

"Now then!" barked the professor as he trained the beam of his flashlight on the book. "It seems that this church is not an *exact* replica of Salisbury Cathedral. There is no crypt in the original church, but there's one in this building, and as you well know, that's where we're going. Hrumph! The entrance to the crypt is behind the main altar at the eastern end of the church. Come on!"

They walked down the middle of the dark church and up a short flight of steps to the altar, which consisted of an oblong block of stone with a bronze cross and two candlesticks on it. Behind the altar Fergie and the professor found a gaping hole in the floor. Near it lay a stone slab and the crowbar that had been used to pry the stone out.

The professor chuckled grimly as he swung the flashlight's beam down into the blackness. "Well, well, well!" he said. "These workmen have been extremely helpful to us, so far. Maybe they had work to do down there. There are stone steps too! How very convenient! Look out below, you ghosts and goblins! We're coming down!"

Fergie glanced skeptically at the professor. He knew why his friend was being so loud and joking. He was scared. But Fergie said nothing. He just got a firm grip on the handle of his searchlight and followed the professor down into the blackness. Fergie counted thirty-nine steps until they reached the bottom and walked onto a slippery marble floor. It was very dark, but the searchlight showed a long whitewashed tunnel that stretched away into the distance. Slowly they began to move along. After every few steps the professor would stop and play the beam of his small flashlight over the walls on both sides of them. Fergie saw that there were white marble tablets set in the walls. Each one was about three feet square and had a name carved on it. Fergie didn't need to be told that there was probably a coffin behind each slab. He read some of the names: ULYSSES THEODORE WINDROW *1858–1910*; SYMPHOROSA WINDROW *1882–1920*; UTHER TINTAGEL WINDROW *1838–1900*.

"Here they all sleep, the members of the nasty and sinister Windrow clan," muttered the professor. "As you can see, some of them died before this church was built, sometime between 1900 and 1909. Old Zeb must've dug the bodies up out of whatever cemetery they were planted in, so he could bury them here. Yuck! What a weird old patootie he must've been! I wonder where *his* tomb is. . . ."

The professor's voice trailed off. He had stopped before a black doorway that was set in one of the side walls of the tunnel. The arch that framed the doorway was made of veined reddish marble, and on the lintel was a carving that showed a jawless skull between two hourglasses. Below the skull was a stone banner with some Latin words on it: PENETRANS AD INTERIORA MORTIS.

"Heavenly days!" exclaimed the professor, taking a step backward. "I knew Zeb was an odd duck, but this really takes the cake! Can you imagine anyone putting up a doorway like this in a family tomb? The Latin phrase means *penetrating to the heart of death*. It's not the sort of thing you normally find inscribed in a crypt. I wonder . . ."

Again his voice died away. He moved the light a bit to the left, and saw a greenish bronze plaque with a fancy scrolled border. The plaque said:

In the Lower Crypt are interred
the remains of
Ensign U. T. French
Mr. Elijah Rehoboam Windrow
Miss Ursula Tench Windrow
Rev. Zimri K. H. Windrow

"Hey!" Fergie exclaimed. "There he is! Ensign French!"

The professor shivered a little. An icy draft was coming from the black doorway, and it made him feel uneasy. Actually, he was more than just uneasy—a strange panic was rising inside him. He did not want to step down into that freezing darkness—but he knew that he was going to. The thought of Johnny lying still and cold under a white sheet made him summon up all his cranky courage. He had to go down there, if all the legions of hell were blocking the way.

"Well, Byron," he said in a voice that trembled, "are you . . . ready?"

Fergie grinned and shrugged carelessly. "Yeah, sure, I'm ready if you are. But the way the air feels, this's more like a walk-in cooler than a burial vault. Maybe it's the place where the workmen keep their beer cold."

The professor said nothing. He strode forward boldly and flashed his light into the yawning black pit. Broad, worn steps stretched away before them. After a brief hesitation they started down. The flight of stairs began to curve to the left almost immediately, and it turned into a spiral that wound around and around endlessly. The farther down they went, the colder it got, but there was something more than cold here—there was an evil, brooding stillness that weighed on their hearts, filling them with despair. Fergie wanted to say clever, witty things, but they stuck in his throat. The professor just stumped doggedly on, moving his flashlight mechanically back and forth. After many turns and countless steps, they passed under a low arch and came out onto a flat, gravelly surface. A dark, empty space opened up all around them, and the searchlight's beam moved over a forest of white pillars. Fergie gaped, and so did the professor—these pillars did not seem to be hand hewn; they were more like stalagmites in a cave, and they sparkled like snow. Fergie moved the beam up, and he saw that the pillars widened out at the top and merged with the ceiling, which was made of the same white, glittery stuff as the pillars.

"My Lord!" said the professor in an awestruck voice. He stepped forward, moving his light over the rough floor they were standing on. Glimmering patches of ice lay among the columns. "Byron," he went on in a wary, nervous voice, "there's something very wrong here. This is not a crypt. It's a cave, and . . ." He paused and stepped forward, wet his finger, and swept it across one of the columns. Then—to Fergie's amazement—he put the tip of his finger in his mouth.

"Hmm . . . *hah!*" said the professor as he licked his lips. "Exactly as I thought! These are pillars of *salt!* And that ceiling overhead is a salt dome. We're surrounded by tons and tons of good old sodium chloride! How about that?"

Fergie was utterly dumbfounded. "Then . . . then how come that sign said this was a crypt? What the heck's goin' on, anyway?"

"I'd really love to know, my friend," said the professor quietly. As he spoke, his breath spewed out in clouds—it was cold, bitterly cold. "I do know one thing, though," he added, turning to Fergie. "This place has a very evil feel, and if we are smart, we will just turn around and skedaddle as fast as we can."

Fergie nodded—he didn't need to be persuaded. Together they started back up the steps. As they climbed, Fergie was amazed at how tired he was getting. Sweat streamed down his face and he was gasping for breath. *It shouldn't be all this hard,* he thought, *it really shouldn't! I'm in pretty good shape. Maybe it's the air or something. . . .*

Fergie stopped. He had to, or he was going to collapse.

"How're . . . you doing?" gasped the professor as he struggled up to the step that Fergie was standing on.

"Don't . . . even . . . ask!" muttered Fergie. He set

down the tool bag and wiped his face with his sleeve. "How . . . how much farther is it . . . anyway?"

The professor shrugged. "Your guess is as good as mine. I think we must be almost there. I mean, we really didn't come down *that* many . . ."

The professor's voice died away, and he looked at his flashlight. To his horror, he saw that the light was slowly fading, the bright glare dwindling to a yellow pinpoint. Fergie's light was going out too. They stood dead still in the darkness. Suddenly they heard a rushing, booming sound that came from far above. The sound grew steadily louder—it was like a violent wind roaring through the staircase tunnel. Something hurtled past Fergie and the professor, flinging them against the tunnel wall. Fergie's searchlight flew out of his hands and clattered against the rough stone. The tool bag and the professor's flashlight went rolling noisily along with it. The booming sound faded out into the distance and was gone. Then silence fell, and two figures lay still on the cold steps.

CHAPTER TEN

It was a long time before either Fergie or the professor moved. Finally Fergie dragged himself to his feet. His legs felt wobbly, but his head was clear. The professor was struggling to stand up. Fergie heard him snort and swear under his breath. That was a good sign—if he was in a lousy temper, that meant he was okay.

"By the old Harry!" the professor growled. "Something came past us like an express train, but . . . but what on earth was it? And where are our flashlights?"

Fergie knelt down and groped on the hard, flinty steps. Finally his hands closed around the old sealed-beam searchlight. He fumbled for the switch, and after jerking it back and forth several times, he got the light to come on. But it was a pale, yellowish glow, not the usual dazzling-white ray.

"Hey, what's wrong?" muttered Fergie. "It's not workin' the way it's s'posed to!"

"This is an evil place, that's what's wrong!" snapped the professor. "I think that the sooner we clear out, the better, so if you can help me locate my flashlight and the tool bag, we'll be on our way."

A few steps farther down they found the tool bag, lying on its side. Near it was the professor's flashlight. After banging it a bit, he got it to come on, but it cast only a weak beam. Up the winding steps the two of them slogged, and after a few more turns they finally made it to the top. The vault with its square tomb slabs was not a terribly cheery place, but Fergie and the professor were very glad to see it. And they were delighted when ―quite suddenly―their lights began to burn more brightly again.

"What . . . what d'we do now?" Fergie gasped as he stumbled out into the long, cool tunnel.

The professor set down his tool bag and mopped his forehead with his sleeve. "I wish I knew," he said wearily. "Ensign French's tomb was supposed to be down in that evil hole, but it is clear now that that sign was set up to deceive us. It's a blasted lie!" The professor began to grow tense and angry, but he forced himself to calm down. There was still a chance that Ensign French's tomb might be here somewhere, and if it was, they had to find it. Fergie and the professor plodded down the length of the tunnel, flashing the beams of their lights over the ghostly white marble tomb slabs. At the far end they stopped before a slab that stood about two feet above the level of the floor. It read:

ENS. ULYSSES THEODORE FRENCH

1873–1909

Ensign French Is the Boss

"Crowbar, please," said the professor grimly as he held out his hand.

Fergie dug his hand into the satchel and came up with the small crowbar. With a muttered curse, the professor snatched it from him and began prying at one side of the slab. Almost immediately it began to move. The professor slid the bar up and pried a little more, and the slab fell forward out of its niche. Springing nimbly backward, the professor let the slab crash on the tunnel floor. He raised his flashlight and looked. There was nothing behind the slab but gray granite blocks, firmly mortared together. The tomb slab had been a fake.

"Well, that's about it, isn't it?" said the professor bitterly as he turned and started walking back toward the entrance to the vault. "There's nothing to do but go back to that wretched hotel and while away the rest of the evening. Tomorrow I suppose I'll have to call up Johnny's grandparents and . . . and see how he is." The professor's voice was beginning to crack, and he seemed to be on the verge of crying. Fergie glanced at him sympathetically. He liked to pretend that he was tough, but he felt awful right now.

"It's okay, professor," he said in a choked-up voice. "I mean, we tried, didn't we?"

"It's *not* okay!" muttered the professor through his teeth. "And if you don't mind, I don't want to talk right now. Let's just clear out."

They went up the steps and down the length of the dark, echoing church. When they opened the side door and stepped out, they saw that the fog had all blown away, and the stars were out. The cold air felt good after the clammy closeness of the church's crypt, but fresh cold air couldn't revive the spirits of Fergie and the professor. They felt miserable and defeated. They got into the car and drove off, and neither one of them said a word until they pulled into a parking place in the Van Twiller town square. Gloom hung over them like a mantle of fog.

Back up in their hotel room, Fergie and the professor did what they could to cheer themselves up. They felt very dirty, and decided to bathe. Since they couldn't agree who'd go first, they flipped a coin, and the professor won. While the old man scrubbed and sang bits of Latin hymns, Fergie stripped off his clothes and put on his bathrobe. He went to the tool bag, unzipped the top, and took out the book on heraldry that he had removed from Zebulon Windrow's library. Sitting down on his bed, he turned on the lamp and began to leaf through the pages. The book turned out to be fairly interesting. Fergie was nuts about history, and he had always been fascinated by the strange designs that medieval knights wore on their shields. The book had pages of full-color illustrations showing many different designs and naming each one. Some of the names were pretty silly: There was *checky* and *gyronny*, *paly wavy*, and *barry dancetty*. Fergie couldn't help laughing at these names, and he began to wonder if there were designs called *jumpy-bumpy* or *dipsy-doodly*.

Finally the bathroom door opened and the professor came out. He was amused to see that Fergie was reading the heraldry book, and he sat down on the bed for a second to peer over his friend's shoulder. In one corner of a page the professor noticed a shield that was quite famous: It showed three silver lilies on a dark-blue field. This was the shield that the kings of France had used at one time. But there was an older shield, that French kings had carried into battle way back in the Middle Ages. What was it called? The professor tried to remember, but the name wouldn't come. And just as he was about to open his mouth to ask Fergie if he knew, Fergie slammed the book shut and made a beeline for the bathroom.

When Fergie lowered himself into the tub, the hot water felt wonderful. He soaped himself and hummed, and closed his eyes and tried to imagine that everything was all right. But then he thought of Johnny, and gloom descended on him again. Their great mission had failed, and now Johnny was probably going to die. Fergie felt absolutely helpless. What could he do? What could *anyone* do? He thought about the dead dog, and the nightmarish salt caves, and the fake tomb of Ensign French. There was something evil out at the Windrow estate, something that seemed to be lurking in the shadows and laughing at them. Was there a ghost? He didn't know, but he did know that every clue they had followed had led them to a dead end. They had lost, and they might as well pack up and go home.

After he had finished his bath, Fergie put his terry-cloth robe on and padded back to the bedroom. The professor was in his pajamas, sitting at the oval table near the window. He had set up his peg chess set, and he had pulled up a chair for Fergie.

"Greetings, Byron!" said the professor, smiling sadly. "Well, here we are, the two would-be explorers. We didn't do so well, did we? But as they say, tomorrow's another day, and maybe during the night one of us will have a brainstorm and solve the riddle of Ensign French and the Urim and the Thummim. Until then I suggest that we play chess. There's nothing more that we can do tonight."

Fergie won the first two games, but the professor was pretty good at chess, and he came back to win the third. By that time it was pretty late, and the professor began to yawn a lot. He decided that it was time to hit the sack. But Fergie was not sleepy yet, so he sat up in the easy chair by the window and read the book on heraldry. Time passed. It was almost midnight when Fergie happened to turn his head and glance out at the deserted town square below. Deserted? Well, not quite. Not far from one of the benches, a man was standing. He was near the edge of a pool of lamplight, so Fergie really couldn't get a good look at him. But he looked old, and he had gray hair that hung down to his shoulders. He's probably just an old bum, thought Fergie, and he was about to go back to his book when something else attracted his attention. The old man was standing very still, and he seemed to be staring straight up at the window Fergie was looking out of. And by some trick of the lamplight, the old man's eyes were glowing red. Fergie shuddered, and he stared hard. Then he closed his eyes and turned away, and when he looked again the old man was gone.

When Fergie woke up Sunday morning, bright sunlight was streaming in through the windows and he could hear church bells ringing. The professor was sitting in the chair by the window, and he was wearing his blue pin-striped suit. In his hands was a small paperback edition of *Five Tragedies by William Shakespeare*. The professor was really wrapped up in the book, and he never noticed when Fergie stared at him and coughed two or three times to get his attention. Finally the professor looked up, and he smiled faintly.

"Oh, hello, Byron," he said in a vague, dreamy tone. "Can I help you with anything?"

Fergie didn't know what to say. Should he tell the professor about the old man with the glowing eyes? He decided not to. Fergie liked to think that he was a tough kid who didn't scare easily. If he told the professor that he had been frightened by an old bum, the professor would kid him, and Fergie did not want that. Then he thought about Johnny again, and—in spite of being a tough guy—he found that he was having trouble keeping back the tears. "What . . . what the heck are we gonna do, professor?" he asked in a cracked, weary voice. "Do we just pack up an' go home, or what?"

The professor laid the book down on a table. He took off his glasses and pinched the bridge of his nose. "You would ask hard questions like that, wouldn't you?" he said with a wry chuckle. He put his glasses back on and glared defiantly at Fergie. "I'll tell you what we are *not* going to do, in case you were wondering," he said in a voice that rose steadily in pitch. "We are *not-going-to-give-UP!* The Urim and the Thummim are out there at that rotten estate, and we are going to find them if we have to tear Zeb Windrow's church and his mansion down *stone by stone!*"

The professor paused. He saw that his ranting had startled Fergie, so he forced himself to smile in a reassuring way. "Look, Byron," he said in a milder tone. "I didn't mean to take your head off, but I'm just as angry and frustrated as you are. When you woke up a minute ago, I was trying to forget about my troubles by reading Shakespeare. But it seems that everything I read leads me back to the puzzle of Ensign French. I was reading *Othello*, and at the very beginning of the play Iago calls himself an *ancient*. I had forgotten what the word meant four hundred years ago, so I glanced at the footnotes, and I saw this." The professor picked up the book and read aloud: "*Ancient: ensign, the third officer in a company of soldiers.* So *ancient* meant *ensign* at one time. Isn't that interesting?"

Fergie shrugged. "Yeah, I guess so. But like my mom says, what does that have to do with the price of fish?"

The professor chuckled. "It may not have anything to do with anything, but it set me to thinking. And my thoughts led me off along some rather strange paths. All of a sudden, I started to wonder: Could it be that there never was an Ensign French at all?"

Fergie's mouth dropped open. "*Huh?* What are you talkin' about?"

The professor paused dramatically. He reached into the inner pocket of his suit coat, took out a box of Balkan Sobranie cigarettes, plucked out a black-and-gold cigarette, and lit it. "What am I talking about?" he said, cocking his head to one side and smiling weirdly. "Just this: All the information we have about Ensign French comes from the guidebook that Charley Coote sent away for. The guidebook was made up by the group of people who bought the Windrow estate. And where did *they* get their information? From old Windrow family records, records that were probably kept by our friend Zebulon himself." The professor paused and took a drag at his cigarette. "We have not found the tomb of Ensign French—right?" he went on, in an excited tone. "All we found was a fake sign, a door leading to some ghastly caves, and a false tomb slab. So I ask you—isn't it possible that Ensign French never existed? What if old Zeb made up all that stuff about a naval officer who married into the Windrow family?"

Fergie's brain was whirling. He began to wonder if maybe the professor's mind had been affected by the frightening adventure that they had had in the salt caves under the church. "Hey, prof, that's really batty!" he said at last. "I mean, why would anybody make up somethin' like that?"

The professor wrinkled his nose. "I can only think of one reason, my friend: Old Zeb wanted to make it harder for us to find the Urim and the Thummim. Think of it this way: If there isn't any Ensign French, then we have a word puzzle. The key to the puzzle is in the name *Ensign French*, or in one of those phrases that are painted on windows or carved on walls at the estate: *Ensign French Is the Boss, Ensign French Is the Unfortunate Traveler*. Do you follow me?"

Fergie jumped out of bed. He paced up and down, bit his lip, and thought hard. Suddenly he whirled and pointed a finger at the professor. "I follow you, sure!" he said excitedly. "But what if you're wrong? What if Ensign French is buried someplace else on that estate? Upstairs in the church, or out on the back lawn, or . . . or maybe they cremated him an' his ashes are in a vase on the mantelpiece in that big old house. Couldn't that be true?"

The professor sighed and nodded glumly. "It could

indeed be true," he said. "You have found a big fat hole in my clever explanation. We may just have to go over the whole estate with a fine-toothed comb till we find where they've buried dear sweet Ensign French. Argh! The thought of doing all that exploring makes my bones ache." With a sudden motion, the professor ground out his cigarette in an ashtray on the table. He sprang to his feet. "Byron, I am sick and tired of chewing over this Ensign French business!" he announced as he brushed some lint off his coat sleeve. "Let's go for a walk on this lovely Sunday morning! Get some clothes on, and I'll meet you by the statue of the fireman in the middle of the town square in about ten minutes. All right?" Without waiting for an answer, he dashed across the room and out the door, slamming it behind him.

A few minutes later Fergie arrived at the town square. He was wearing a plaid shirt and corduroy trousers, and his hair was neatly combed. On a bench at the base of the statue sat the professor. He was reading a news-paper and humming quietly to himself. Pigeons were strutting on the grass, and groups of well-dressed people strolled by on their way to Sunday-morning services.

"Ah, my friend, you have arrived at last!" sighed the professor, putting down his paper. "Byron, you look resplendent! And you will be fascinated to know that there is a Catholic church over on the far side of the square—I asked the desk clerk, who seems to know everything. Will you go along with me? I know your folks are Baptists, but . . ."

Fergie shrugged. "I'll go. Far as I'm concerned, one church is just as dull as the next one—but don't tell my mom I said that, or she'd take my head off!"

The professor got up and led Fergie across the sunny square. Beside a row of chestnut trees stood a red-brick church built in the Gothic style. The sign outside said ST. MARGARET'S CATHOLIC CHURCH, and there was a list of Mass times. They were just in time for the ten-o'clock service, so they went into the dark, cool church. The professor paused inside the door to dip his fingers in the holy-water font and make the sign of the cross.

"We seem to be spending a lot of our time in churches these days," he whispered. "Perhaps it will make us more holy."

Fergie snickered, and a middle-aged lady who was passing turned and glared at him—apparently she didn't approve of laughing in church. Taking Fergie by the arm, the professor led him into a pew near the back of the church, and the two of them sat down to wait for the service to begin. Minutes ticked past. Fergie took off his watch, wound it, and put it back on. The professor fiddled with his Phi Beta Kappa key and looked around. On their left was a row of tall stained-glass windows, but as far as the professor was concerned, they were not terribly interesting. The glass was dull green and yellow and smeary brown, for the most part, and at the bottom of each window was a square plaque that told who had donated it. The professor let his eyes wander. Hmm . . . down the aisle a bit was a window with a shield in the middle of it. The shield was like the one the professor had noticed in the heraldry book. It had silver lilies on a blue background, but instead of having just three lilies, this shield was covered all over with lots of tiny lilies—the whole design was like a wallpaper pattern. Suddenly something clicked inside the professor's mind. This was the ancient French shield he had been trying to remember the name of. All right now, what was the name? It was . . . it was . . .

"*Holy H. Smoke*," roared the professor, and he stood straight up in the pew.

He had done it! He had figured it out!

CHAPTER ELEVEN

"By the eternal powers!" the professor crowed, swinging his fist in the air. "I *knew* I could figure it out, and I did!"

Everybody in the church turned and looked at the professor. Alarmed, Fergie jumped up and started pushing the professor out of the pew.

"Come on, for gosh sake!" he whispered excitedly. "We gotta get outa here! They'll call the police or somethin'! Come on!"

The professor was still grinning like a fool as he sidled out of the pew and walked quickly out of the church, followed by Fergie. Halfway down the sidewalk, the professor turned and grabbed Fergie by the shoulders.

His eyes were wild and bulging, and his face was getting very red.

"Byron!" he exclaimed breathlessly. "Don't you understand? I *did* it! I was right when I guessed what old Zeb was up to! *Ensign French* isn't a person, it's a code! Do you want to know what it means?"

Fergie was thoroughly alarmed by now. He had been worrying lately that the professor might be losing his marbles, and now he was sure of it. But he had heard that you ought to humor crazy people, so he forced himself to smile politely.

"Uh . . . that's nice, sir," he said nervously. "Why . . . whyn't we go back to the hotel an' . . . an' talk? Okay?"

The professor let go of Fergie's shoulders and gave him a disgusted look. "Oh, come off it, Byron!" he growled. "You think I've flipped my lid, so you're trying to be nice to me till you can call the boys with the white coats. But I'm *not* insane, and if you'll give me five seconds, I'll prove it to you!" He took a deep breath and let it out. "Look," he began, holding up his forefinger, "while we were in that church, I saw a shield in one of the windows. The shield has a name, and it's called *France Ancient*. You follow me so far? Good! Well, earlier this morning I was reading Shakespeare, and—as you may remember—I mentioned that *ancient* used to mean *ensign*. So if you take the name *Ensign French* and change the first part of it, you get *Ancient French*, don't you? And if you flip-flop that name, you get *French*

Ancient, which is almost the name of the blue shield with the silver lilies all over it. Do you see?"

Fergie felt a bit dizzy after this explanation. "Yeah, I . . . I guess so," he said slowly. "So do we hafta go back to that church out at the estate an' look for a shield like the one you saw in this church here?"

"Yes," said the professor, nodding solemnly. "That is exactly what we have to do. Heraldic shields are often used as decorations in old churches, and we will have to hunt until we find the right one. We'll go out there tonight, but first I think we'd better go back to the hotel room and do a little planning. Also, we'll give the Dixons a phone call to find out how Johnny is getting along. Come on."

Fergie and the professor walked quickly across the square to the hotel. They paused in the lobby to use the pay phone, but the Dixons didn't answer.

"They're probably down at the hospital with Johnny," said the professor glumly as he hung up. "I don't know what that means, but—for the time being—we'd better try to keep the poor lad out of our minds. We have to concentrate on other things."

At a little after seven o'clock Fergie and the professor were standing outside the huge old stone church on the grounds of the Windrow estate. They were both dressed in their scruffy "exploring" clothes, and near them on the ground was their tool bag. As Fergie fiddled with his searchlight and shone the beam around, the professor puffed on one last cigarette. When it was finished, they were going into the church to hunt for the *France Ancient* shield. Overhead the stars shone, and a chilly night wind was blowing. It rustled the leaves of an oak tree that grew next to the mansion.

"You know somethin', prof?" said Fergie thoughtfully. "That shield we're lookin' for might not even be in the church. It might be someplace else."

The professor grimaced and blew smoke out through his nose. "I know, I *know!*" he muttered irritably. "There isn't any logical reason why we should be looking for the shield in the church. If it exists at all, it might be in the mansion, or even in that little round temple over there in the woods. But the church seems to be a good place to start. Any objections?"

Fergie shook his head.

"Good!" snapped the professor, and he threw his burned-out cigarette to the ground and stamped on it. "I think that at last I am ready to — Oh, no! You don't suppose, do you, that . . ." The professor's voice trailed off, and he dropped to his knees quickly. As Fergie watched in bewilderment, he unzipped the top of the tool bag and plunged his hand inside. "Double phooey!" growled the professor as he stood up again. "I left both of my stupid flashlights on the backseat of the stupid car! How could I have *been* such a nitwit! Well, I guess I'll just have to go back and get one of them."

Fergie gave the professor an exasperated look. He had been living with this cranky old man for three days now, and he was beginning to get fed up. "Aw, come on, prof!" he said. "Are you gonna go all the way back to the car just to get a dinky little flashlight? This one here's all we need!"

The professor took a deep breath and let it out. He was trying very hard to keep from losing his temper. "Byron," he said in a strained voice, "I know you think your searchlight is the greatest invention since the wheel, but my old nickel-plated flashlights are perfectly decent, and I've used them for over twenty years. I like them, and we may need them both before we're through. It'll only take us about three minutes to scoot out to the car and get one little bitty flashlight. We'll be back here before you know it. How about it?"

But Fergie was feeling stubborn. He folded his arms and turned away. "You go ahead if you want to, prof!" he muttered sullenly. "I'll just wait here for you. I'm not scared of the dark. Go on."

The professor stared at Fergie in sheer exasperation. "Byron," he said, "have you flipped your wig? Think of the strange things that have happened to us out at this place. We oughtn't to split up—it'd be very dangerous! Come on with me."

Fergie glared defiantly at the professor. He knew in his heart that the old man was right, but he did not want to give in. "Nah, you go ahead," he said with a careless shrug. Then he added, "Why don'tcha leave me the holy water bottle? If any monsters come outa the woods to get me, I can spray the stuff at 'em. You know, like Black Flag insect spray? C'mon, just give me the bottle."

The professor clenched his fists. "Oh, very *well*!" he growled, and he plunged his hand into the pocket on the front of his sweat shirt. He pulled out the plastic bottle and handed it to Fergie. "Here! Hang onto this! I'll be right back."

Snatching the searchlight from Fergie's hand, the professor stomped off into the darkness. For a few minutes Fergie stood watching the spotlight's beam as it bounced along the ground. Then the professor passed behind some trees and the light was gone. Fergie was alone. Whistling softly, he paced back and forth for a few more minutes, and then he sat down on a stone bench that stood near the church. He turned the holy water bottle over in his hands, and he laughed. *Holy water!* The idea of spraying this stuff in the face of some ghost was . . . well, it was just too funny for words. For a while Fergie had believed in ghosts and the magical Urim and Whatsis, but now his skeptical side was coming out. Fergie told himself that all the things that had happened out here could be explained. Even the rushing wind and their flashlights acting funny . . . those things might be caused by electromagnetic forces, or X rays. He began to wonder why he had ever let the professor drag him along on this trip anyway. There wasn't anything to find out at the cruddy old estate, and suppose they did discover something, it wouldn't—

Suddenly Fergie sat up straight. What was that? What had he heard? It was a thin wailing sound and it seemed to be coming from the dark grove of trees that grew near the little stone temple. There it was again! With a shock, Fergie realized it was the professor's voice, calling for help. Yes, there was no mistake about it. But what was the professor doing over there? Why wasn't he out at the car, getting his flashlight? As Fergie sat wondering, he heard the cry again. *Fergie! Help me! Help!* With that, Fergie sprang to his feet. He dropped the holy water bottle onto the bench, and he started to run.

"I'm comin', professor!" he yelled. "I'm comin'! Hang on!"

Across the grass he pounded, arms swinging, legs pumping up and down. It was not hard to see where he was going, because the moon was rising and the sky was full of stars. In no time at all Fergie was at the edge of the dark grove. He found the white flagstone path and began to pick his way along it. All around him the trees were rustling, but he did not hear the professor's voice anymore. At the foot of the steps that led to the bronze doors, Fergie stopped. He could not see very well in this place, but it looked as if one of the doors was ajar. Could the professor be—

"Help! Fergie! Come here!"

Fergie's eyes grew wide. It was the professor's voice,

calling from inside the temple. With a wild yell Fergie dashed forward. He leaped the short flight of steps in one bound and threw his weight against the half-open door. Groaning loudly, it moved inward, and Fergie plunged into the darkness. Then he stopped.

"Professor!" he called. "Hey, prof, where are you? Are you okay?"

No answer. Then, suddenly, all around him, Fergie heard the hum and rustle of insects. They were buzzing furiously and brushing their wings over his face. Frantically, Fergie began to wave his arms, but the insects were all over his body, and then—suddenly—they were gone.

Fergie was panting now, and sweat was pouring down his face.

"Professor?" he said in a weak, throaty voice. "Are you . . . ?"

Fergie's voice died. Something had stepped out of the darkness in the center of the room. It was short and stooped, and it wore a robe with a hood, and it looked like the statue on the outside of the temple. Tentacles reached out from the long sleeves, and they whipped around Fergie's arms, gripping them tightly. He was being dragged forward, and the sagging hood opened wide. Fergie's head was thrust into the darkness inside the hood, and something like a large, slimy suction cup was plastered over his face. He couldn't see, he couldn't scream, and his breath was cut off. Frantically he thrashed and kicked, but his struggles soon grew weaker, and as he started to lose consciousness, a voice in his brain kept saying, *You're gonna die, you're gonna die, this is what it feels like, you're gonna die.* . . .

CHAPTER TWELVE

When Fergie woke up, he was lying on the grass outside the little grove of trees. The professor was kneeling over him and sponging his face with a wet handkerchief.

"Wha . . . wha . . . how . . ." mumbled Fergie as he struggled to sit up. "Where'd you . . . I mean . . ."

"Good evening," said the professor dryly. "So you have decided to stay alive. Good! Would you mind telling me what you were doing near that filthy, accursed temple? You were supposed to wait for me by the church."

Fergie was fully awake now, and he was getting angry. "*Me!*" he exclaimed. "*I* was s'posed to wait for *you!* I came runnin' over here because I heard you yellin' for me! And I don't mind tellin' you, I wondered what you were doin' here, instead of bein' out at the car gettin' your wonderful, stupendous, precious flashlight."

"I did go out to get the flashlight," said the professor quietly. "But when I tried to get back in through the gatehouse, the door was locked. I hammered and kicked at it, but I couldn't get in. So I had to start the car and bring it over and park it next to the wall, so I could use it to climb up. I made it over the wall, but by the time I got back to the church, you were gone." The professor sighed. "You know, my friend," he went on, "it was a very lucky thing for you that I found the holy water bottle lying on the bench. And it was also very lucky that I came over here to search for you. I thought that you might have come here to bury that dead dog. Well, when I arrived at the temple and saw that the door was open, I became very worried, and then I heard a sound of scuffling that seemed to be coming from inside. I rushed into the temple with the holy water bottle in my hand, and I saw you struggling with that evil hooded thing. I was scared out of my mind, but I had the holy water, and that did the trick. A few drops and our hooded friend shriveled up and vanished."

Fergie clutched himself and shuddered convulsively. Then he wiped his arm across his face. "What was it, professor?" he asked. "What was that thing with the tentacles?"

The professor glanced at the handkerchief that he had

been using to wipe Fergie's face. It had a bad smell, so he flung it away. "It was a familiar," he said. "Old Zebulon Windrow was a wizard, and he had the power to conjure up familiar spirits, demons from the hellish pit. Sometimes these familiars take the shapes of cats or other small animals, and sometimes they take the shapes of monsters. That thing that attacked you was like somebody's bad dream, but it had the power to kill."

Fergie thought a bit. Then he shook his head and smiled ruefully. "I promise you one thing, prof," he said. "I won't ever kid you about your holy water again. I thought I was gonna end up like . . . like . . ." He shuddered again.

"Like the dog?" said the professor grimly. "You might have. That was certainly what somebody wanted. It was no accident that the gatehouse door was locked. Some evil intelligence is at work here, and it wanted to split us up. Are you ready to go back to the church with me?"

Fergie nodded emphatically. "I sure am! What d'we do next?"

The professor grinned and helped Fergie to his feet. They walked back slowly, and soon they were standing by the stone porch on the south side of the church. Moonlight shone down on the bench where Fergie had been sitting not so long ago. And next to the bench was the leather valise with their tools in it.

The professor handed the searchlight to Fergie. Picking up the tool bag, he clicked on his own flashlight and shone the beam into the shadows under the porch. "If infernal powers have not sealed up this door," he said, "we will go have ourselves a look inside Zeb's church. Are you coming?"

Fergie nodded. In silence they stepped in under the elaborately carved arch. Holding his breath, the professor twisted the iron ring, and the door opened. Into the church they went, and once again the cavernous dark space opened around them. Fergie could see the vague shapes of arches, and a glimmer of moonlight in one of the far-distant windows.

"Impressive, eh?" whispered the professor. "I wish we had time to just wander around, but I'm afraid we have to stick to our business. Would you lend me your searchlight? It's a lot stronger than my little flashlight, and I need it to peer at the nooks and crannies high up on the wall. Byron, why are you glaring at me that way?"

Fergie was furious. He had almost gotten killed when the professor went back to get his precious flashlight, and now he was saying that he couldn't use it! But Fergie swallowed his anger. He gave the professor the big red lamp, and took the small flashlight from him. They padded slowly down the aisle, and the long beam of the searchlight crept along the wall. Up, down, it moved, and it poked into the dark hollows under arches. As he went, the professor began to whistle softly. It was a weird sound to hear, in this empty church, at night. Fergie said nothing. He moved the beam of his flashlight over the pavement, hoping that he would find the lily-covered shield before the professor did. But he didn't find anything, and neither did the professor.

Suddenly, with a loud, crabby exclamation, the professor stopped. "Of *course!* How could I have been so dense! *Ensign French is the BOSS!* Of course! What an idiot I have been!"

Fergie did not have the faintest idea of what the professor was talking about. It sounded like he had figured out something, but it was hard to tell what. "Huh?" he said. "What's up?"

The professor cackled. "Well you may ask what's *up*! Have a look for yourself!"

As Fergie watched, the beam of the searchlight climbed the stone wall and moved out across the ceiling overhead. It was a curved, arched stone ceiling, and directly above the place where they were standing was a stone disk with four raised ribs running away from it, like this:

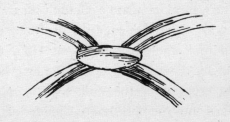

"You see that disk up there?" said the professor. "Well, it's called a *boss*. In Gothic churches, those bosses are often carved into fantastic, grotesque shapes. And sometimes they have shields on them. And *that*, my fine friend, is what we've got to look for! Follow me!"

The professor took the binoculars out of the tool bag and hung the strap around his neck. Then he started to move slowly along, whistling softly. Fergie followed the professor, who was now playing the searchlight beam straight up over the ribbed ceiling. They walked down the side aisle of the church and then turned right and moved along the nave, which is the main body of a church. Fergie got to see lots of bosses, and they all seemed to have decorations; but the bosses were so far away that it was hard to tell what the decorations were supposed to be. Every so often the professor would stop and ask Fergie to hold the light steady. Then, with the aid of the binoculars, he would peer and squint a bit, grumble, and move on. As they crept along, Fergie found that he was getting more and more nervous. This vast, dark old building was really giving him the creeps—even more than it had the first time he was in it. He kept imagining that he heard tiny sounds, like footsteps or muffled coughing. But each time he stopped and strained to listen, he heard nothing.

"Professor, I hope we can find what we came for an' get outa this place!" he muttered. "I'm gonna get the screamin' woo-hoos, but good, if we stay here much longer!"

"I'm not feeling terribly calm myself," muttered the professor as he maneuvered the light beam along the ceiling. "It may be just nerves, but I have this funny idea that there is somebody here in the church with us. Somebody who hates us. On the other hand, I'll be darned if I'll be scared away by anybody or anything until— Aha! By the holy and invisible powers, I think we've found it!"

Fergie looked up. Far above, on the ceiling, was what appeared to be a stone disk with a painted shield on it. The beam of the searchlight hovered over the shield, and Fergie could see little silver blobs on a background of midnight blue. Excitedly, the professor lifted the binoculars and peered up.

"*Hooray!*" he whooped. "They *are* lilies! Hooray for the lilies of France Ancient! We've found it, we've found it!"

As Fergie watched in amazement, the professor danced a little jig on the church floor. But in the middle of his dancing, he stopped. Angrily, he snapped off the searchlight and cursed loudly.

"Blast! Wouldn't you know it! There's *always* something that can go wrong!"

Fergie didn't know what to say. "Huh? I . . . I thought everything was okay. Isn't it?"

"Oh, sure! Everything's just ginger-peachy!" growled

the professor sarcastically. "Everything's fine, except for one little bitsy detail: We're down here, and the shield is up there! *How in the devil are we going to get up to it?*"

Fergie's heart sank. He glanced up again. He understood in an instant what the professor meant. The ceiling over their heads was very high, too high to be reached even with a stepladder. If the professor was right, the Urim and the Thummim were under the shield. But at this distance they couldn't do any poking or prying—they could only stare.

Fergie set down his tool bag. He felt like crying, but he fought back the tears. There had to be *some* way! While the professor stood fuming and swearing in the darkness, Fergie moved the beam of the small flashlight around . . . and then his heart leaped. Not far away, a scaffold had been set up. It was made of crisscrossing steel pipes, and boards had been laid across the top to make a level platform. The scaffold was a tall one—it reached almost all the way up to the ceiling. Unfortunately, it wasn't right under the stone disk—but it just might be close enough!

"Hey, professor!" Fergie exclaimed, tugging at his sleeve fiercely. "Look! It's absolutely perfect. Look at what I found!"

"What is it now?" asked the professor wearily. He was still sunk in despair.

"It's a . . . *whatchamacallit!*" said Fergie excitedly.

"I mean, it's . . . a scaffold-type thing, the kind painters use . . . you know! C'mon! Look at it!"

The professor turned his head and looked. And then he brightened up immediately. "Oh, my!" he exclaimed delightedly. "I see what you mean! Yes, I certainly do! Byron, you are a genius, an absolute genius! Bring the tool bag—we're going up!"

A steel ladder was bolted to the side of the scaffold. Once again the two of them switched lights—this was done so that the professor would have both hands free to climb. Fergie hooked the handle of the searchlight into his belt, and with the tool bag in one hand he started up. When he got near the top, he threw the bag onto the platform and pulled himself up after it. Fergie heaved a deep sigh of relief—he had made it! But then he realized that he had not heard the professor climbing behind him. Where was the old man, anyway?

"Hey, professor!" Fergie called. "Come on up! Are you okay?"

A voice answered out of the darkness below. "I'm all right, but I'm afraid my poor old flashlight has had it! I was looking around for a mop handle or something to poke at the disk with, and I dropped the stupid gizmo, and now the switch won't work! Shine your light on the ladder, and I'll be up in five sec—"

From deep below the church came a long, ominous, rumbling noise. The floor shook, and the scaffold creaked and swayed.

"Good lord, it's an *earthquake!*" exclaimed the professor in a shocked voice. "We've got to get out of here! The whole bloody building is going to come down on our heads!"

CHAPTER THIRTEEN

For ten terrifying seconds Fergie and the professor waited. Then the shaking stopped and the noise died away to a distant grumbling.

"My stars!" gasped the professor. "What was *that*?"

"You got me!" said Fergie. He leaned out over the edge of the scaffold and pointed the beam of the searchlight down onto the ladder. "I dunno what that was, but you better climb on up here so we can get what we came after an' then clear out! C'mon, professor! *Hurry!*"

For a second more the professor hesitated. Was it right for him to risk his life and Fergie's in a building that might come down on their heads at any minute? But they were so close to the end of their search, so very, very close . . .

"Hang on, Byron!" the professor called. "I'll be up in a jiffy!"

A few minutes later the professor was squatting on the end of the scaffold with Fergie. In his hands he clutched a broom, and as Fergie held the searchlight steady, he began to prod at the shield with the handle. Now that they could see it up close, Fergie and the professor realized that the shield was not painted on the stone. It was a piece of metal held in place by bolts. As the professor prodded, the shield made a tinny whanging sound.

"What're you tryin' to do?" asked Fergie.

"I'm . . . trying to loosen the piece of tin . . . if I can!" muttered the professor, and he lunged again with the broomstick. "It would help if the scaffold were closer to our target, but it isn't!" After a few more blows, the professor paused and squinted at the shield.

"Drat!" he growled. "We haven't done a thing to it, except dent it a little!" The professor paused. The corner of his mouth was twitching, and he seemed to be thinking. "Byron!" he snapped suddenly. "Is there a screwdriver in that tool bag of ours?"

Fergie unzipped the bag and fumbled around inside with his hand. "Yeah . . . here it is!" he said at last, holding up a long screwdriver with a chipped red wooden handle.

"Thank you!" said the professor. "That will do nicely! Hang on to it a minute, will you?"

As Fergie waited, the professor laid the broom down

on the scaffold. He took off one of his sneakers and pulled the shoelace out of it. After showing Fergie where to point the light, he took the screwdriver from him and began to bind it to the broom handle.

"Good . . . and *tight!*" grunted the professor as he worked. "I learned to wrap and frap in the army, many years ago, and I still know how, it seems!" Finally he stopped and held the broomstick up. The screwdriver was bound tightly to the end, like the point on some caveman's spear. "All righty now!" said the professor, as he grasped the broom handle in both hands. "If you will point the beam up there, so, Byron . . . ah! Perfect! *Now* let's see what we can do!"

There was a thin black line between the edge of the shield and the stone. Was it a space that could be widened? The professor meant to find out! Carefully, he slid the tip of the screwdriver into the dark crack and began to pry. *Squeeeek.* The gap widened, and a metal bolt fell out. They heard it hit the floor below with a tiny *ping.* But the strain of prying had knocked the screwdriver askew, and the professor had to haul it back, lay it on the boards, and refasten it. He fussed and fumed as he retied the shoelace. . . . Ah! It was tight again! With a triumphant growl, the professor raised the stick and went to work on the shield. The shadowy gap was wider. In went the point and the shank of the screwdriver, all the way up to the handle. The professor pried outward with the broom handle, and they heard a quick sliding noise. Something had been sitting on the underside of the shield, and now it zipped out, and with a *tock!* it hit on the pavement stones below.

"Hah!" exclaimed the professor as he glanced down into the darkness. "We've got the prize in the cereal box, whatever on earth it may be! Point your light down there, Byron, and . . . no, on second thought, forget it! Let's just climb down and glom the thing and get out of—"

The rumbling started again, and the scaffold jerked back and forth as if a giant were shaking it. Panicked, the professor pitched the broom handle over the end of the scaffold and started shuffling on his knees toward the ladder. As Fergie tried to hold the light steady, the professor started down. The rumbling grew louder, and the scaffold vibrated. Its steel legs danced and chattered on the pavement, and the professor had to cling tightly to the rungs of the ladder to keep from being pitched onto the floor below. A short way from the bottom he jumped, and he landed on his feet.

"Throw me the light, Byron!" he yelled in a panicky voice. "I'll hold it for you so you can climb!"

But Fergie was already on his way down, with the handle of the searchlight clenched in his teeth. As soon as he got to the bottom, he took the light in his hands and waved the beam over the floor. There it was! A small package wrapped in brown paper and tied with twine.

"*I'll get it!*" roared the professor, and he lunged forward, dropped to his knees, and scooped up the package.

The floor of the church began to heave and pitch, like the deck of a ship in a storm. The professor staggered to his feet and reeled sideways as another shock hit. At the other end of the church things were crashing—it sounded as if parts of the ceiling and walls were coming down.

"Oh, good Lord! Oh, good heavens!" babbled the professor as he glanced wildly around. "We've got to get out! Come on, follow me!"

The professor dashed down the length of the church and Fergie ran after him. The steady rumbling went on, broken now and then by crashes. The professor really did not know where he was going, but he raced on in a blind panic, hoping that a door would appear. They had come to an open space lit faintly by moonlight. It was the well underneath the central tower, and if they had turned to their left, they could have gotten out through the door they had entered by. But the professor was not thinking clearly, and neither was Fergie. Together they galloped off into the shadows, and Fergie's wildly swinging light picked out a narrow, pointed door.

"*There!*" yelled the professor. "Out through there! Come on!"

He rushed at the door and opened it, and now the two of them were climbing, single file, up a narrow spiral staircase. Up and up it wound. The walls vibrated and hummed, and bits of mortar dust sifted down onto their heads. Still they climbed. Finally they came to a little hallway with two tall, narrow windows set in one wall.

The bottom of each window was about chest high to Fergie—it would not be hard to climb out of it. However, there were lots of little square panes of glass set in strips of lead.

"Bash it!" screeched the professor, gesturing wildly toward one of the windows. "Use the searchlight! Go on! What are you waiting for?"

Fergie hesitated a second, and then he swung the heavy lamp. Glass crunched, and the lead strips bent. Again and again Fergie swung the light, and each time more glass broke. Standing on tiptoe, he reached up and, with his elbow, smashed out the twisted strips of lead. There was a ragged hole now in the bottom part of the window.

"I . . . I think we can get . . . out now," Fergie gasped, wiping his hand across his sweaty face. "Here . . . take this!" He shoved the searchlight at the professor. Amazingly, it was still working.

Clutching the light in one hand and the package in the other, the professor watched as Fergie scrambled up into the window opening. Poking his head out, Fergie took a look around. By the light of the full moon he saw a slanted roof about fifteen feet below. Fergie glanced to the right. The ridgepole of the roof was the closest perch they could find, and they could reach it by edging along the side of the tower wall below. There was a molding, a lip of stone that they could stand on, but they would have to flatten their bodies against the wall and slither sideways like a couple of sticky-footed lizards. Fergie wondered if they could do it. For the moment, the church had stopped shaking, but if it started to quiver when they were clinging to the wall outside . . .

"Byron, what are you doing?" rasped the professor. "We've got to get out of here before this thing comes down on our heads!"

Fergie was in agony—he couldn't make up his mind. Probably they ought to just turn around and go back down the stairs and try to get out of the building some other way. But he thought of the narrow staircase and what would happen if they were trapped inside when the church started to collapse. If they were outside, they'd have a fighting chance. . . .

Turning to the professor, Fergie explained quickly what they'd have to do if they went out through the window. The professor swallowed hard and turned pale —he was pretty limber for an elderly man, but could he play Human Fly on the outside of this tower? The tower gave a sickening lurch, and the rumbling started again.

"All right," he said hoarsely. "You go first—I'll follow."

Fergie clambered out through the window opening. Carefully, he eased himself down, feet first, onto the ledge below. Moving slowly, he edged over to the left until he was where he wanted to be. Below him was the upside-down V of the roof. If everything worked out right, he would end up sitting on the high point. So he lowered himself until he was kneeling on the ledge, and then slid gently down until he was straddling the copper-sheathed roof. Fergie didn't dare look down—he knew that there was a drop-off on either side of him. He glanced up, and to his amazement he saw the professor inching along the wall above him. Fergie edged himself back along the roof and soon the professor was kneeling above him, ready to drop down. Fergie held his breath. Would the professor slip and fall? A second later there he was, astride the roof like a rider on a horse.

"Hah!" snorted the professor triumphantly. "That was nothing, nothing at all! I must fit wall climbing into my morning exer—"

All around them things started to happen. The steeple shook and swayed as if it were made of rubber. The tower vibrated, and pieces of carved stone fell off it. Then the church collapsed. It seemed to sag and dissolve, like an old hotel that has been dynamited. The steeple leaned lazily over and smashed on the eastern end of the church, and amid a long-drawn-out roar the ruined building settled down, down, down. Terrified, Fergie and the professor clung to the roof and closed their eyes and prayed. They expected to be crushed at any second by tons of stone, and Fergie kept hoping that he would be knocked unconscious quickly. But finally the unearthly noise stopped, and Fergie and the professor opened their eyes. The roof they were sitting on was now almost level with the ground. It was as if the church had fallen into a gigantic hole. Choking clouds of dust rose around them, and it was hard to see, but they were alive.

"Well, wasn't *that* fun!" growled the professor. "Come on, Byron, we'd better skedaddle! In five minutes every fire engine for miles around will be here, and the police, and heaven knows who else! Let's vamoose!"

The two of them went down the roof on their rears, as if it were a children's slide. They picked their way out over fallen stones and raced toward the front gate. When they got there, they saw that the earthquake had brought down a big section of the wall, and that made their escape easy. They felt exhausted and light-headed, but happy. Fergie threw himself across the hood of the car and laughed helplessly for a long time. Then an awful thought struck him—had they left the paper-wrapped package behind?

He straightened up and looked at the professor, who was leaning casually against a fender and lighting a cigarette.

"Professor!" Fergie exclaimed breathlessly. "Hey, professor! Did you . . . I mean, did you remember to . . ."

The professor turned. On his face was a smug, superior smile, and now Fergie could see the bulge in the front of his jacket.

"Byron," said the professor as he blew smoke out through his nose, "what kind of idiot do you take me for? I'm afraid your wonderful sealed-beam searchlight is gone forever, and so is the tool bag and one of my sneakers. But I did remember *this*!" He patted the bulge and grinned toothily. After another thoughtful puff he opened his mouth to say something else, but he froze. In the distance a wailing sound had started.

"Oh, good gravy!" he exclaimed, flinging his cigarette away. "The fire trucks are on their way already! We'd better go, or they'll think we were the ones who wrecked their lovely church. Can you imagine spending the rest of your life in a jail in the town of Van Twiller? What a repulsive thought! Come on, Byron! Time's a-wasting!"

CHAPTER FOURTEEN

A few minutes later Fergie and the professor were roaring back, full speed, toward the town of Van Twiller. As they careened around a turn, they passed two fire trucks going the other way. Their sirens were screeching full blast, and the firemen waved at the professor's car as he drove past.

"Hey, professor?" asked Fergie, after the siren had died away. "How come they sent fire trucks? I mean, it's not a fire, it's a building smash-up, isn't it?"

The professor grinned. "When you get older, Byron," he said, "you will discover that they send the fire engines for *any* kind of disaster, whether it's a kitten up a tree or a general conflagration. By the way, I'd love to know what exactly *did* happen to that church. Those caves underneath—perhaps they were structurally weak in some way. Hmm . . . this will require some thought!"

"Well, while you're thinkin', could you pass me over the package?" asked Fergie eagerly. "I wanna see what's in it!"

"So do the rest of us!" snapped the professor. "And I'll thank you to keep your grasping hands to yourself till we get back to the hotel. Then we *both* can have a peek!"

As they walked through the lobby of the Van Twiller Hotel, Fergie and the professor felt very embarrassed. They looked absolutely, positively a mess: Their hands were cut and bleeding, their clothes were torn, and they were covered from head to foot with grayish dust. And, of course, the professor was limping along on only one shoe.

"We're amateur cave explorers," the professor announced as they stopped at the desk to get their room key. "And I'm afraid we had a small accident—but that's life!"

The clerk stared at the bedraggled explorers as if they had just dropped in through the ceiling. But he didn't say anything—he just gave the professor his key and turned hastily away. Once they were upstairs, with the door bolted, the two of them quickly washed their hands and faces. Then, while Fergie watched, the professor laid the mysterious parcel on the bed and began undoing the string that fastened it. In a few seconds he had the paper off, and before them lay a leather-covered jewel case about four inches long. With trembling fingers the professor opened the lid. The case was lined with blue plush, and stuck into the cushion were two old stickpins, the kind that men used to wear in their neckties. One had an opal on the end, and as the professor turned it back and forth in the lamplight, it seemed to change: One moment it was all blue shimmers, the next all fiery orange depths. The other stickpin was less dramatic: It simply held two small, cloudy rock crystal knobs with brass bolts stuck through them. The knobs swung from a little hook on the end of the stickpin.

The professor carried the case with the pins over closer to the lamp. He pulled them out of the plush and held them up, turning them back and forth. At first Fergie had felt awestruck, but now he was getting doubtful. His grandma had once shown him some pins that looked a great deal like these. But Grandma's pins were only a hundred years old. How could these pins be the objects that the Israelites had used, thousands of years ago?

"I know what you're thinking, Byron," said the professor as he ran his fingers over the smooth surface of the opal. "And it certainly is true that these doohickeys don't look terribly ancient. The metal parts of the stickpins are probably not much more than eighty years old, but the two crystal knobs and the opal could be a lot older. They could well be the Urim and the Thummim. We won't know until we try to use them to make Johnny better—and speaking of which, we had better stop oohing and aahing and get ready to hit the road. Are you ready for an all-night drive back to Duston Heights?"

Fergie's mouth dropped open. He hadn't realized that the professor would want to start back right away. "Can . . . can we do it?" he asked in a stunned voice.

The professor shrugged carelessly. "I don't see why not. It's only ten P.M., and I'm certainly not sleepy—I'm so excited that I could jump out of my skin! If we leave soon, we ought to get back around three in the morning. The sooner we can get these things to Johnny, the better —and let us hope and pray that we are not too late!"

As quickly as they could, Fergie and the professor got ready to leave. They changed into clean clothes and stuffed everything else into their suitcases. When he was all dressed and ready to go, the professor slid the case with the stickpins into an inner pocket of his suit coat.

"*There!*" he said, giving one last look around. "Are you all packed up, Byron?"

"Sure!" said Fergie jauntily. "Let's make ourselves scarce!"

In the lobby downstairs the professor paused to pay for the room they had used. But as he was taking the money from his wallet, he noticed that the clerk was eyeing him suspiciously.

"We've been called back by an emergency," said the professor, smiling as politely as he could. "I hate to drive at night, but it will be necessary, I fear."

The clerk went on glowering. "When you was out

cave explorin'," he said, "I don't suppose you did any o' your explorin' out at the Windrow estate?"

The professor gave him a blank look. "No . . . no, we didn't," he said. "Why do you ask?"

"Why do I ask?" answered the clerk. "Oh, no special reason. Only the church out there fell down 'bout half an hour ago. Jist wondered if you saw it happen."

The professor pretended to be shocked. "The *church* fell down? You mean the one with the great tall steeple? Well, I *never*! I wish I could stay to talk, but we really are in a hurry. Good evening to you." And with that he snatched up his suitcase and bolted out the door, with Fergie close behind him.

Out in the town square a commotion was going on. People were talking excitedly in little groups, and police cars zoomed past, their red lights flashing. In the distance more sirens wailed. Ignoring all this, the professor and Fergie threw their suitcases into the car, got in, and drove off. All night they roared across New York, Connecticut, and Massachusetts, and at a little after three A.M. they pulled into a parking space outside the hospital in the city of Duston Heights.

"What do we do now?" asked Fergie as the professor turned the motor off.

The professor glanced at his face in the rearview mirror and smoothed down some hairs on his head. "We are going to have to try to get in," he said. "I don't think there's any point in trying to argue with the head nurse or whoever is on duty at the main desk. At this hour she will merely assume that we are a couple of escaped lunatics and throw us out. Sooo . . . it will be necessary to sneak in. Are you with me?"

Fergie grinned and nodded. He liked the idea of a mad dash through the hospital at three in the morning—it sounded exciting. He got out of the car, closed the door quietly, and followed the professor up the long, curving walk that led toward the main entrance of the hospital. Halfway up the walk the professor stepped off into the shrubbery that grew nearby. After a quick glance ahead, Fergie saw why he was doing this: The main doors of the hospital were made of glass, and anyone inside could easily see two people who were coming up the walk. Moving as quietly as possible, the two of them shoved their way through fir boughs until they were near the entrance. Then the professor tiptoed forward and cautiously peered in through the glass. The lobby of the hospital was empty, but behind the reception desk a stern-looking nurse was sitting. She was reading something on a clipboard.

"Is the coast clear?" Fergie whispered.

"No, it's not," the professor hissed. "Have patience— we'll get in *somehow*!"

So they waited. After what seemed like hours, the nurse got up, laid the clipboard down, and moved away from the desk. The professor held his breath—he wanted to give the nurse time to get out of the room. Finally, when he was sure she was gone, he motioned for Fergie to follow him. In a few swift strides they were inside the door. They raced across the lobby toward a white door marked STAIRS. Up the steps they ran, until they emerged into the second-floor corridor. The hospital was deathly still. An electric clock buzzed over a desk that was set in a little alcove, but there was no one there. As Fergie and the professor moved down the hall, their shoes made a squidgy sound on the slick linoleum. They stopped outside the door of Room 203. Fergie's heart was pounding, and they were both sweating hard. Quickly the professor grabbed the knob and opened the door. They both stepped inside.

A tiny blue night lamp burned on the wall, and by this faint light they saw Johnny lying in his bed. He was under an oxygen tent, so they couldn't see his face very well, but his limp, pale hands lay on the blanket. The professor moved to the head of the bed, and with trembling hands he peeled back the plastic tent. Johnny looked the way he had the last time the professor saw him: His eyes were closed, and his half-open mouth was curled into an ugly sneer. As Fergie watched, the professor took the jewel case from the inside pocket of his suit coat. He snapped the case open and pulled out the two stickpins. After laying the case down on the edge of the bed, he reached forward and pressed the opal and the two crystal knobs against Johnny's forehead. For a full minute he held them there, while he muttered a prayer. Fergie held his breath and watched. Would it work?

Nothing happened. No change came over Johnny. Again the professor pressed the jewels to Johnny's forehead, and again he prayed. But Johnny still looked the same, and his eyes stayed closed.

"Oh, my God," the professor breathed. "I was afraid of this. We have failed."

"Are you sure?" asked Fergie.

"Yes, I'm sure. We'd better leave. We've done all that we can do."

With a sinking heart the professor folded the tent back down over Johnny. He put the two stickpins back in their case and shoved the case into his pocket. Then, just as he was turning away from the bed, the door of the room opened. There stood the stern white-haired nurse, the one who had been sitting at the main desk. For a moment she said nothing. She just stood there with her hand on the knob, staring at the two intruders.

Finally she spoke. "And may I ask," she said in an angry, shocked voice, "what on earth you two are doing in this patient's room at three o'clock in the morning?"

The professor swallowed hard. He tried to act calm, which was difficult under the circumstances. "I . . . we . . . I mean, my friend and I, here, we just returned from a long car trip, and we wanted to see young John Dixon at once." The professor folded his hands and glanced nervously around. His explanation had not been very good, and he knew it. He braced himself for an outburst of anger.

But the nurse stayed calm. She glared at the two of them for a few more seconds, and then she motioned for them to step out into the hall.

"I don't know what sort of crazy people you two are," she said as Fergie and the professor filed past her, "but I'll tell you one thing—you are very lucky that I'm not going to call the police. But I *will* call them if you are not out of this building in two minutes. Do I make myself clear?"

Fergie nodded silently. So did the professor. After another hate-filled glare, the nurse stepped back into Johnny's room and shut the door. Fergie and the professor stood there a few seconds longer. Then they turned slowly and began to walk away. But they had not taken more than four or five steps when the door of Johnny's room opened again and the nurse stepped out into the hall. On her face was an awestruck look.

"Wait!" she called. "Wait, please!"

Fergie and the professor turned. What was going to happen to them now?

The nurse took a step forward. "Are . . . are you Professor Childermass?" she asked in a frightened voice.

The professor nodded. "Yes," he said stiffly. "Why do you ask?"

"Because Johnny's awake, and he wants to talk to you."

The professor looked totally stunned. He smiled faintly and fiddled with his watch chain. "Hrmph! He

. . . he does, eh? Well, I'll be glad to talk to him in a second, but . . ."

His voice trailed off. Turning away, the professor took two steps down the hall and then he stopped. Putting his hands to his face, he began to sob uncontrollably. It had been a very long day.

CHAPTER FIFTEEN

On a lovely warm Sunday in late May, Johnny and his friends were riding on one of the swan boats in the Boston Public Garden. The swan boats are long, shallow barges with rows of park benches on them. At the back of each one is a large metal hollow swan, painted white, and inside each one sits a park employee who makes the boat go by pumping pedals. The boats go around a long duck pond that is divided into two parts by an old stone bridge. As the man pumped the pedals, Gramma and Grampa Dixon sat in the rear seat of one of the boats, munching popcorn and talking happily. In the row in front of them sat Professor Childermass, Professor Coote, Fergie, and Johnny. Johnny was pale, but color was beginning to come back into his cheeks. He had been out of the hospital for only a couple of weeks and he was still a bit unsteady on his legs, but he was in a cheerful mood. At the moment he was eating a hot dog and listening to Professor Coote, who was explaining—once again —why the church on the Windrow estate had fallen down.

"Okay, professor," said Johnny as he threw a piece of hot dog bun to one of the ducks that were swimming around the boat. "I think I've got it straight—some of it, anyway. The church fell down because the salt caves underneath collapsed, and they collapsed because water got in and dissolved the pillars of salt that held up the roof of the caves. But how did the water get into the caves?"

Professor Coote smiled placidly. "The water got in through a channel in the rock of the riverbank. The Hudson River had been eating away at a weak place in the rock for years, and finally river water began to seep into the caves. The whole shebang might have collapsed earlier this year, except for one thing: On the banks of the river, at the bottom of the hill that the Windrow estate was on, there was a different kind of cave. It was just a narrow slit in the limestone, and its entrance was hidden by some bushes, but a team of explorers discovered it about a year ago. They went slithering in on their bellies, and guess what they found. Their cave connected with the underground river channel. I've done a drawing for you that'll help explain the setup. Here—have a look."

Professor Coote reached into his inside jacket pocket and pulled out a folded piece of paper with a pencil drawing on it.

"The explorers made their way to the place where the channel entered the salt caves," Professor Coote went on, "and it didn't take them long to figure out that there'd be a disaster if they didn't find some way to keep the river water out. So they went and reported their terrible discovery to the people who owned the estate, and—"

"Wait a minute!" said Professor Childermass, interrupting. "Wait just a teeny little minute! There's a staircase leading down from the crypt of the church to the salt caves—or rather, there *was* a staircase before the church fell down. If people went down the stairs, wouldn't they have noticed that water was seeping into the caves?"

Professor Coote smiled wryly. "Roderick," he said, "I'm glad you brought that up. It may come as a shock to you, but the staircase and the marble doorway *never existed*! I was looking through the foundation's guide-book the other day, and it doesn't say anything about any staircase to the caves. Don't you think it would have mentioned a weird unlikely detail like that? I would guess that the ghost of Zebulon Windrow put that doorway and those stairs there so you two could have a peek

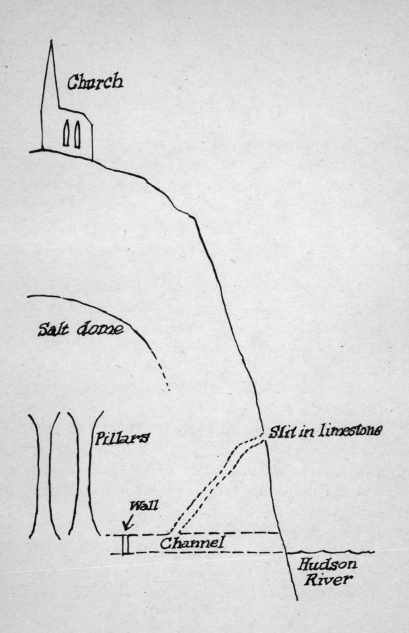

at those evil, haunted caves. But I'll say more about old Zeb in a minute."

"Okay, okay," said Fergie impatiently. "So the cave explorers told the owners of the estate about the caves and the water seepin' in. Did they panic? What happened then?"

"What happened? Why, the owners paid the explorers to go back and plug up the end of the channel with a little wall of stones and mortar. It was a tedious job, but they managed to do it, and the wall was right here, where I've drawn this little arrow on the map. Do you see it?"

Johnny blinked and nodded. "Yeah, I understand. So did an earthquake knock down the wall? Is that what happened?"

"Earthquake, my eye!" said Professor Childermass scornfully. "That's the official version, but what really happened was this: Old Zebulon Windrow got up out of his grave and went down to smash the wall and let the water in. I know that sounds very unlikely, but I am convinced that that's what happened!"

Johnny's eyes grew wide. "*Really?*"

Professor Coote sighed. "Yes, I'm afraid so. You see, right after the church collapsed, the estate's owners sent the explorers down into the cave again, to see if they could figure out what had happened. Well, when the explorers had made their way to the place where they had built the wall, they found something rather unpleasant: A big hole had been knocked in their wall, and lying near the wall was a skeleton dressed in the rotting remains of an old-fashioned suit. After digging through some old dental records, the estate's owners were able to say that the skeleton was Zeb Windrow's." He smiled sourly. "Zeb had been buried in the Lady Chapel at the eastern end of the church, and everyone assumed that the body had plummeted down into the caves along with all the other rubble. But after hearing Roderick's tale, I would have to agree with his conclusion: The skeleton was down there *before* the church collapsed, and it had gotten there under its own power. Remember the evil wind that knocked Fergie and Roderick over when they were climbing back up from the caves? That was old Zeb on his way down."

Johnny gasped. On a bright sunny day in a crowded park, it was hard to believe in walking corpses. "Really?" he said again. "Are you sure, professor?"

"Reasonably," said Professor Coote, pursing up his lips and staring owlishly at Johnny. "Remember, old Zebulon was the head of a clan of witches and wizards, and he was the one who owned the Urim and the Thummim, the magic objects that gave the Windrow family their powers. When he died, he never really died completely. His spirit hung around, guarding the family treasure, and it had the power to make itself visible. Byron here saw Zebulon standing in the town square of Van Twiller one night, though he didn't realize that he was looking at a ghost. Later, when our two friends started poking around in the old church, old Zeb decided to make their search a tiny bit harder for them. He probably thought it'd be fun to have the church come down on their heads, just as they had found what they were looking for."

"Fun, fun!" said Professor Childermass bitterly. "If I had the old creep here, I'd show him what fun was—I'd wring his skeletal neck! But in spite of everything, we did solve his insane puzzle, and we got away with the wonderful and exciting prize! By the way, Charley, are you going to notify the museums and the other archeologists of your find? Are you going to get rich and famous and all that?"

Professor Coote laughed. "Not likely, Roderick, old boy! Not likely! You're forgetting how skeptical scholars are. If I take those stickpins to the archeologists at Harvard and try to tell them that they're looking at the Urim and the Thummim, they'll decide that good old Charley Coote has finally gotten a bit soft in the head. What proof do we have? None. Of course, I could go around trying to work magic with the stickpins, but magical objects are dangerous: They don't always do what people want them to do. So, my friend, we'll have to forget about fame and fortune and making miracles happen. We've got what we want, anyway, don't we?" He turned to Johnny and patted him on the shoulder.

The two professors beamed at Johnny, and he acted

embarrassed, as he always did when people fussed over him. Silence fell, and the boat passed under the bridge and began to glide around the odd little stony island where the mallards build their nests in the spring.

"What *are* you guys gonna do with those ridiculous stickpins?" asked Fergie at last. "I mean, I'd really like to know."

"We'll stick them in *you* if you keep asking questions like that!" grumbled Professor Childermass good-naturedly. "Actually, to be serious, I think we ought to put them on a shelf somewhere and forget about them. Or I could try to get them to do something useful for me, like help me to give up smoking."

"It would take a major miracle for *that* to happen!" said Professor Coote, laughing. "You will probably be smoking your last cigarette as they lower you into your coffin."

"Are you trying to suggest that I don't have any will-power?" asked Professor Childermass, pointing an accusing finger at his friend. "Well, just you watch!" He reached into his coat pocket and pulled out a black-and-gold cardboard box. Opening it, he showed everyone that there was only one cigarette left. Then, with a grand flourish, he flung the cigarette away. It landed on the island, and a squirrel that was crouching nearby scampered up to it, nosed it curiously, and then began to eat it.

There was a stunned silence.

"That's *impossible!*" Fergie exclaimed. "Squirrels don't eat cigarettes!"

"They eat candy cigarettes," said the professor calmly. Reaching into his other coat pocket, he took out another cigarette box, opened it, fished out a real cigarette, and lit it while everyone laughed.

JOHN BELLAIRS

is the critically acclaimed, best-selling author of many gothic novels, including *The House with a Clock in Its Walls; The Figure in the Shadows; The Letter, the Witch, and the Ring; The Curse of the Blue Figurine; The Mummy, the Will, and the Crypt; The Dark Secret of Weatherend*; and his latest tale, *The Spell of the Sorcerer's Skull*. Mr. Bellairs has also written a number of adult books, among them *The Face in the Frost*.

A resident of Haverhill, Massachusetts, Mr. Bellairs is currently at work on another suspense thriller.

FROM THE SPOOKY, EERIE PEN OF
JOHN BELLAIRS . . .

☐ **THE CURSE OF THE**   15429/$2.75
    BLUE FIGURINE

Johnny Dixon knows a lot about ancient Egypt and curses and evil spirits—but when he finds the blue figurine, he actually "sees" a frightening, super-natural world. Even his friend Professor Childermass can't help him!

☐ **THE MUMMY, THE WILL**   15323/$2.50
    AND THE CRYPT

For months Johnny has been working on a riddle that would lead to a $10,000 reward. Feeling certain that the money is hidden somewhere in the house of a dead man, Johnny goes into his house where a bolt of lightening reveals to him that the house is not quite deserted . . .

☐ **THE SPELL OF THE**   15357/$2.50
    SORCERER'S SKULL

Johnny Dixon is back, but this time he's not teamed up with Dr. Childermass. That's because his friend, the Professor, has disappeared!

More Fun More Adventure More Magic

☐ **15348 DANCING CATS OF APPLESAP**
by Janet Taylor Lisle   **$2.50**
Only Melba Morris, age 10, knows that the 100 wondrous cats who dance the days away in Mr. Jiggs' drugstore are really . . . a miracle.

☐ **15350 OWLS IN THE FAMILY**
by Farley Mowat   **$2.25**
There's nothing two owls named Wol and Weeps can't do—from turning the whole household topsy-turvy to shaking up the entire neighborhood!

☐ **21129 THE WIND IN THE WILLOWS**
by Kenneth Grahame   **$1.95**
When Rat and Mole and Badger and Toad get together for a series of outrageously silly adventures, the fun never stops.

☐ **15349 THE OWLSTONE CROWN**
by X. J. Kennedy   **$2.50**
When Timothy and Verity Tibbs follow a tiny ladybug private eye over a moon-lit path to Other Earth, magical adventures happen fast.

☐ **15317 JAMES AND THE GIANT PEACH**
by Roald Dahl   **$2.95**
James, sadly resigned to a life of misery with two wicked aunts, rolls instead into a truly wild adventure . . . inside a giant magical peach!

You can order these books today.

Prices and availability subject to change without notice.